# Crepes

This is a work of fiction. Names, characters, places and incidents are the products of the author's imagination or are used fictitiously. Any resemblance to actual events or people, living or dead, is coincidental.

Copyright © 2020

All rights reserved. No part of this publication may be reproduced or transmitted in any form or by any means, electronic or mechanical, including photocopy, recording, or any information storage and retrieval system, without permission in writing from the publisher.

ISBN-9798672098876

Printed in the United States of America
First edition 2020

"Something supersedes thinking, despite its truly awesome power. When existence reveals itself as existentially intolerable, thinking collapses in on itself. In such situations-in the depths-it's *noticing*, not thinking, that does the trick. Perhaps you might start by noticing this: when you love someone, *it's not despite their limitations. It's because of their limitations.* Of course, it's complicated."

~ Dr. Jordan B. Peterson

# Contents

Chapter 1..................5

Chapter 2..................13

Chapter 3..................24

Chapter 4..................34

Chapter 5..................46

Chapter 6..................57

Chapter 7..................68

Chapter 8..................79

Chapter 9..................90

Chapter 10..................98

Chapter 11..................109

Chapter 12..................117

Chapter 13..................126

Chapter 14..................130

Chapter 15..................138

Chapter 16..................145

# Chapter 1

Sweat builds up on the crease of my forehead. With every step I take on the crimson track my legs begin to hurt a little more, but somehow I'm getting a boost of energy running and putting every one of my limbs to work. As the sun burns down on me and some other girls who are staying after practice, my thoughts begin to take over and I'm in my head rather than on the campus of California state college. *You can do this Candace, you can do this, last mile and you're almost at five minutes. Sarah with the bright red face is behind you come on Candace. Sarah said your tennis shoes are cute. Well, she can look at the back of them.* I get out of my thoughts when coach Pearson becomes visible in his red tracksuit furrowing his thick black brows and staring down at his stopwatch that some days is my enemy, and others, when I'm on my A game, my best friend.

"Come on Candace, you're almost there!" Coach Pearson shouts with his strong Caribbean accent. Even though I've already ran for a good 40 minutes on and off during practice I push myself to go a little harder making my heart beat faster and faster.

I'm approaching the last 100 meter when a familiar face makes me break my focused stare. Leaning against the fence that separates the track from the silver bleachers is my best friend that's not a piece of metal that times me. Her name is Sofia. She's looking at her head of medallion curls in her pink compact mirror that she always tells me is better than the camera app on her smartphone. Her blue eyes move from the mirror and look at me as I run past the place where she's standing.

"Come on Candace!" she shouts as if she's trying to make everyone walking by turn and look at her. I keep on running and hustling, a little faster thanks to Sofia who is now jumping up and down. The intensity in my legs makes it seem like hours, but I run to where coach is standing only for Sarah whose whole body is red to go past coach a second before me. *Damn Candace you were so close. How did she get past you?*

"5 minutes 4 seconds! Candace you shaved 4 seconds off good job," coach Pearson says.

"Thanks," is all I can manage to say as I bend over and begin catching my breath. I've been running cross country and track and field 11 years. I started when I was wearing silly bands in middle school and to this day after every run all I want to do is collapse on my bed which is now in my dorm that I share with Sofia.

As I grab my water bottle and gym bag from the side of the track and say goodbye to some of the other girls Sofia runs over to me making her silver earrings dangle. She's always wearing the newest styles of clothes while I'm fine in some track pants and a hoodie.

"Hey sweaty," her high pitch voice squeaks and she throws her arm around my shoulder.

"Hey," I say, still not completely getting all of my breath back. This doesn't stop Sofia from beaming from cheek to cheek, and she continues talking as we walk to the front buildings of campus.

"What's with the face? You were like Usain Bolt out there. I wish I could run that fast. My mile is the same amount of time I spend scrolling through YouTube."

I let a sigh escape from my lips. "Sarah Thompson passed me," I say.

Sofia cocks her head to the side. "The one whose whole body looks like a tomato eating hot Cheetos?" Sofia asks.

I narrow my eyes at her. "Everyone gets red when they run, but yes."

Sofia gains some more pep in her step and I have to speed walk to catch up with her even with her arm around my shoulder. For someone who doesn't work out or have practice 4 times a week her lissome legs sure take her far.

"Don't worry about Sarah, you did not get on the cross country and track and field team because of her." Sofia and I stop walking and she takes a moment to look right into my eyes as she places her hand on my shoulder. She has that glowing smile on her face, but I can still tell the words that are about to come out of her mouth aren't going to be jokes.

"Remember what I told you Candace," she begins, but I don't need her to finish as I've already heard these words many times from her.

With no emotion in my voice I say along with her, "Only compare yourself to your yesterday, not someone else's today." This sappy quote is something Sofia has been saying since I met her at the beginning of the school year. It's cute and all, but really I know she got it from some cheesy magazine that didn't know they were quoting Hemingway. Sofia quickly goes back to being all smiley and the one serious bone in her body disappears.

"Now come on let's eat," she says.

I pull my phone out of the pocket of my shorts to check the time, "It's barely 5pm." Sofia doesn't listen and pushes the glass doors open to the campus cafeteria. This, next to the hallways of the dorm rooms has to be the number one place on campus to hang out. Unlike high school cafeterias it's humongous and filled with decent foods that aren't on brown trays or in foil. The large space is filled with students sitting along the long mahogany tables. No one really seems to be eating and instead hovered over a textbook or typing vigorously on their laptops. Why they choose to study here instead of the Starbucks down the street or the library, I don't know, but Sofia and I begin walking inside.

"So who cares what time it is, I'm hungry." At that I just shake my head. Sofia is always hungry or eating, that noise you sometimes hear in the back of the lecture hall; it is probably her trying to tear open the wrapper to a granola bar. Still I love her though, and I wouldn't admit it to her, but I could use a pick me up after that long practice. As we make our way through the cafeteria Sofia waves to a bunch of people from different groups who happily wave back. I just force a smile. Like most of the many people in this college I don't know all that many of my colleagues, unlike Sofia who gets to know a lot of people in student council.

When she's done waving like a queen or miss universe she turns to me as we reach the many stations of the cafeteria.

"So what are you in the mood for?" I ask.

Sofia scrunches up her face and looks from the taco station to the green juice cart where some girls in yoga pants are hanging out. "Hmm," she says. I'm fine with just getting a protein bar from one of the campus vending machines, but I don't say anything and watch her scan the cafeteria we've been in so many times before. It never changes all that much, but Sofia looks for something new every time.

She squints for a moment and then her eyes light up. "Crepes," she says.

I burst into laughter, but Sofia remains in the same spot looking at the corner of the cafeteria. "What? There's a new crepe station, let's try it." She gestures over to where she was looking at and I turn to look at the abandoned station where there doesn't seem to be anyone working the old dusty cash register. The tables surrounding the station are also empty unlike all the others.

"You've got to be kidding me right?" As the words come out of my mouth a deceiving smirk slips onto Sofia's face. One that in the year I've known her has always been a big red warning sign for trouble.

I slit my eyes at her. "What's the real reason you want to get crepes?" I cross my arms and Sofia's smirk disappears.

She crosses her arms. "I heard they're really good, and I want something sweet." I've known her long enough to tell when her eyebrows arch towards the ceiling she's lying, but I don't object to following her towards the crepe station. Some cheerleaders still in their uniforms get ahead of us in line, and we slowly follow them as they pick through every crepe topping on the worn out menu. Seeing the chocolate syrup drizzled on the crepes by a middle aged server in a bright yellow top makes my stomach growl along with the strong smell of yeast and sugar that lingers around my nostrils. My eyes don't move off the crepes sitting on the other side of the dirty display glass until Sofia nudges me in the ribs.

I turn my head to look at her as we're steps away from the cash register and taking our order.

She leans in and whispers, which is louder than her actual voice. "I'm not a crepe person, but there's this cute guy I want you to meet, he works here." At that all of my attention goes to her and my mouth flies open. She's always trying to get me to meet new people guys or girls.

"Sofia I don't want to meet anyone, I look like crap," I hiss. I try to adjust my baby hairs that keep flying away when the cafeteria doors open before Sofia can try to console me and say I look fine.

"Next," I hear a husky voice say.

Sofia's smile gets brighter, but my skin begins to burn up and I probably look like Sarah as I stare down at my running shoes. "Look here he comes," Sofia whispers. I take a quick look up from my shoes to see the middle age woman working the cashier move and a figure replace her spot.

"I gotta go," I blurt out. You'd think I was standing on the track; I dash past the crepe station and scurry out of the cafeteria. Faster Candace, faster Candace, you gotta go, you gotta go now. These thoughts keep on swarming in my mind until I reach my dorm room and collapse on my bed just like I wanted to do when I got my mile time.

# Chapter 2

I'm only able to get a good 20 minutes of sleep before the dorm door slowly creeks open and Sofia's head pops in. The smell of the rich chocolate follows her as she walks past the messy side of her room where some of her clothes lay on the floor and she sits on the edge of my twin sized bed. I keep my head plastered to my pillow until the rich chocolate smell somehow finds its way to my nose and I turn to look at Sofia. She has two white paper plates in both of her hands and on each sits what I think is a crepe with chocolate and strawberries busting from the sides. I've never been to Paris, let alone outside of the United States, but I'm positive that brown mush is not what crepes are supposed to look like. Still my stomach growls and my mom always told me not to judge a book by its cover.

"Are you feeling better Ms. Track star?" Sofia asks with a hint of sarcasm I know she's not trying to hide. She has that pouty face I used to use with my sisters when I wanted to or rather was forced to apologize.

"I'm fine," I mumble and sit up with my old mattress making all of its old mattress noises.

"People who are fine don't go darting out of the cafeteria like they're a mad person," Sofia says. She places the two white plates that are barely holding up the crepes on the nightstand; which I should mention is only ever clean thanks to me. "But if you're as fine as you say you are, do you forgive me for giving you a panic attack and not telling you about the guy," she says softly.

"I didn't have a panic attack," I argue. Even though I'm not completely sure what caused me to run out of the cafeteria. Sure I didn't want this aforementioned guy to see me post-practice, right after those gorgeous cheerleaders who were ahead of us, but a part of me thinks there is another reason. "It's ok, let's just eat these crepes," I say.

Sofia claps her hands then pulls two white, easily breakable forks out of her bomber jacket. Knowing me and my dislike for food on my bed we move over to Sofia's bed where it smells like ramen noodles and bath and body works perfume.

We sit crossed legged like kindergartners with the plates on our laps and at the same time we stab our forks into the deformed middle of the crepe. The rich chocolate smell gets weirder as it gets closer to my mouth and I take a whole mouthful. *These definitely aren't the same crepes in Paris.*

I try to swirl the bite in my mouth around, but each time I chew the chocolate seems to thicken along with what I think are frozen or out of date blueberries. It takes me a good amount of effort to use all the strength in my mouth to swallow what I hope Sofia didn't pay a lot for.

"Oh my god that was horrible," I say trying to lick the bad taste out of my mouth. Sofia puts her fork back into the crepe and clears her throat in the loudest way possible.

"It wasn't that bad," she says in a high pitch tone.

I raise my eyebrows and look down at the messy crepes on our laps. "Really then take another bite." *This is going to be interesting.* Just saying those words makes me shiver as I think about what I put into my mouth.

Sofia who never backs down from a challenge forces a smile and picks up her fork that's covered in whatever fake chocolate they used to make that insult to deserts everywhere.

"Fine," she says proudly. She slowly raises the fork with the smallest bite of the crepe to her glossed lips, but she stops when it's only an inch away from going in her mouth. "No, I'd rather drink a whole bottle of apple cider vinegar, I mean they're not bad, but they're weird and I just can't handle the taste." She puts the fork back on the mess on her plate and like we're reading each other's minds we both get up and go out into the dorm hallway to dump the plate in the trash. Not wanting to look at the want-to-be crepes anymore we scurry back into our dorm. The second Sofia closes our poster covered door she turns to me with the same smirk she had before we got into the crepe line. "So want to go back to the cafeteria? I don't have a student council meeting."

"No I'm good, I think I'm going to have a late night gym session so I can beat Sarah next time."

Sofia shakes her head as I go over to my side of the pretty small dorm. "You don't need to beat her Candace, especially if it requires doing squats." At that moment I just give Sofia a slight smile and grab my gym bag from where I plopped it down after I collapsed on my bed.

"Thanks but I need this workout, you good here?" I ask while in the process of putting all of my black waves into the same high ponytail.

"Of course I'm good, but are you good?" She raises her eyebrows and kicks off her sneakers sending them flying right beside her pajama pants that lay wrinkled on the floor.

"Why wouldn't I be good?" I try to think about if my period is coming up or if I have some exam to cram for that would stress me out. But there is nothing.

Sofia takes off her magenta bra without even touching her graphic tee before throwing it to the ground. A skill she has mastered very well since we moved in together. As she kicks her bra close to the hamper she hardly ever uses she gets closer to me.

"Because Candace we're 18, freshmen in college, we shouldn't be sleeping for 8 hours or doing extra gym sessions we should be having fun that's why our parents paid so much money to get us here right?" She throws her arms in the air and I just stay in the same place although I want to keep inching towards the door.

I can't help but get defensive. "The gym is fun for me."

Sofia keeps her calm smile, but lets out a big sigh. "I mean like actual no stressing about your mile time fun, that's why I wanted you to meet this guy." Sofia throws some of her curls to the side and takes a breath of the ramen noodle scent lingering in the air.

"Do you even know him Sofia, what if he's a complete psychopath or something?" My hand falls on my hip.

"Trust me I know a psychopath when I see one, and he's not it." Her eyes seem to be sparkling a bit, and as much as I want to object to her trying to set me up when she hasn't even had a long term boyfriend, her smile makes me feel differently.

Losing the stubborn side of my tone I say, "Fine, what's his name? Maybe, I can look up his social media."

Sofia looks away from me and at the Nirvana poster that's close to falling off the beige door.

I slap my hand on my forehead. "You don't know his name do you?"

"I don't," she admits and puts her hands on her hips.

"Sof," I whine.

"But I swear he just has this glow about him that screams I should be in a relationship with Sofie's best friend and roommate." Sweat begins to form on Sofia's face as if convincing me to talk to this guy is becoming hard work for her.

I take a step away from the door that I guess I won't be exiting out of anytime soon. "Are you sure that glow wasn't telling you he should be in a relationship with you." If so I'm pretty sure that glow she's referring to is just sweat and the bright rectangle lights that beam on him when he's serving those horrific crepes.

Sofia bats her eyelashes and a pink hue comes to the top of her cheeks. "Candace come on you know bad boys are my type and this boy is definitely a good one." She isn't kidding. The last boys she had relationships with or in most cases just a hookup had stygian pasts with at least one neck tattoo which sounds too stereotypical, but then again so was Sofie. They gave me shivers, but I have to admit they were pretty good looking whether or not they listened to death metal or were on the verge of suspension. Seeing that I'm still unconvinced, Sofia rests her hands on my shoulders right next to the navy blue stray of my sports bra that may or may not have been hers.

"Candace I know I seem like the crazy manic pixie dream girl who is extremely boy crazy, but really I just want my best friend to experience things besides track and the almost toxic smell of textbooks. Plus I'm not asking you to marry him, I'm asking you to just consider his existence." Sofia's big eyes beg for me to answer and she taps her magenta nails against my skin. She has a point. All she really wanted was for me to meet the guy. I don't know why I'm putting so much thought into it.

"Fine I'll consider his existence, but no more impromptu meetings when I look like crap, okay?" I arch my eyebrows a tad.

Sofia doesn't waste any time to take her hands off of my shoulders and clap her hands as she does a little jump up and down making me notice the glittery polish sparged on her toenails.

"Yay Candace is going to have fun, and maybe you actually living will give me a subject for my short film." Sofia waltzes over to her nightstand and picks up her silver, Sony film camera that was sitting in the middle of her mess of nail polishes and broken hair clips. She puts the camera in front of her face making her look like Quentin Tarantino or Ava DuVernay even though I'm pretty sure the camera is off.

Aside from Sofia's hobbies of thrifting old clothes, following YouTube makeup tutorials, and trying to make me get out of my shell she's majoring in film and wants to make the next Mean Girls or Sixteen Candles. She actually spends more time with her camera in front of her then on social media like the rest of the phone obsessed people in our generation. Sometimes I wish I was like her in the sense that she knows what she wants when she graduates while I just hope track and field takes me somewhere besides the hospital with an injury and great cardiovascular health.

Sofia plays around with her camera some more pretending that I'm some famous Hollywood actress and she's one of those persistent journalists asking me questions.

"Candace Palmer you look so chic where did you get those shorts of yours? And why did you pair them with that under armour tank?" Sofia asks in a deep, almost British accent that sounds like a mixture between Scottish and Dutch.

I respond with the same tone, my accent more Dutch than Scottish. I then do a little twirl in my workout clothes that I probably should've changed some time ago. "I chose them because they are the only ones left in my drawer, don't you love the pink ink stain." I turn so Sofia can see the splatter mark across the bottom of my shorts.

"Oh yes those are so in season, is it paint or an over-use of laundry soap?"

"Bad laundry soap Ms. Stevens."

"Ah good heavens you're beautiful Ms. Palmer, just beautiful." Sofia shouts for the whole hall to hear.

Seeing the green on button and realizing she's actually flustered I cover my face feeling flustered.

"I'm off to the gym now," I say still in the same accent as I wave to Sofia.

"Wait," Sofia yells in her normal voice. She puts her camera back on her bed and begins rummaging under it. After some seconds she pulls out a box of protein bars and throws me one and I catch it.

"Thanks," I say and head out of the dorm.

I plug my earbuds in and walk along campus towards the gym where I'm programmed to go to. As the loud bass of rap music I'm listening to blares in my ears, I can't help, but look across campus that seems to be at its best under the clear blue sky and light rays of the fall sun. The grassy lawn and the many buildings aren't what catches my eye on this walk, and I can't help but look at the couple passionately kissing with every fiber in them. The girl whose hands are around the guy's neck seems so content and safe in the guy's letterman jacket as she looks up at him when their lips depart. Her eyes seem to be sparkling as the guy runs his hand through her bone straight hair and for a second I stop walking and relax my eyes on them. *Hmm maybe Sofia was right. I could use a new experience of some kind.* When the guy seems to almost take his eyes off of the girl's rubescent face I begin walking and continue in the direction of the gym. *Come on Candace, you got to keep going, staring isn't nice.*

# Chapter 3

The next morning I wake up to the smell of the can of ramen noodles Sofia ate last night. I lay in my bed and I can barely move as I'm sore from my thighs to the very tips of my toes. *That late night gym session wasn't the best Idea Candace.* I sit up and run my hands through the tangles of my hair that's still a tad damp from my shower last night. I look over to my side and Sofia is sprawled out on her bed with the ramen noodle can still intertwined with her sheets and her curls just as crazy as my waves; tossed everywhere as she lets out a few snores.

I open up my phone just for the bright light to blind my tired eyes as it tells me it's 6:30 am, also known as too early for a day of college, or doing anything for that matter. After I turn the brightness down I find myself in a spiral of scrolling through my Instagram feed which I don't normally do, but on this Thursday my earliest class, political science, isn't until 9 am. My thumb becomes slightly numb as I double tap pictures of various people who come up on my explore page. Most of the taps just lead to, well I don't even know exactly know what I'm looking at as I quickly scroll past. Most of the pictures aren't what would be considered one's normal feed of Instagram models and are just pictures of my old track friends in tanks and shorts showing off how much they ran.

After I comment on a picture of my friend Nicole who just achieved a 9 second 100 meter I find myself looking at Sarah's profile and my brow furrows at the sight of the eight post on her profile. They aren't pictures of her posing with her Fitbit and tying her sneakers candidly, instead all of her posts are of her smiling with friends or with a cup of coffee. The last post is the one that really catches my eye as it's of her kissing a boy with flaxen ruffled hair that Sarah seems to be stroking as she stands on the tips of his toes. *How does she have time to kiss boys and have a better mile time than me?* I shake my head and go to my profile which is such a contrast as all of my photos are of me in gym clothes with some kind of track medal that I now keep in the top drawer of my dresser. Sure I have one of me and Sofia, but it's after a track meet, and Sofia isn't even doing her full model poses she pulls off on her own social media.

"What are you doing?" Sofia's voice booms. I look up from the still bright light of my phone to see Sofia standing over me in her velvet shorts and oversized t shirt that is similar to the one I'm drowning in. Her hands are on her hips and her eyes are right on my phone and Instagram.

"Nothing," I mumble and quickly exit out of the app. While still looking at her I open my health app which I haven't used since I first got my iPhone.

Sofia snatches my phone out of my hand before I can say another lie and her fingers begin simultaneously tapping on my screen that has one slight crack. I get off of my bed to face her and when my feet touch the cold wooden tiles she shows me my screen which is back on Instagram. *Damn I forgot to exit out of my apps.*

Sofia shakes her head like my mom would. "Snooping on Instagram before getting out of bed, I expected better from you Candace." She's about to hand me my phone but when I move my hand she extends her arm and my phone in the air. I may be more athletic and able to beat her in a wrestling match, but she has at least 3 inches on me making me stand on the tips of my toes that are still not accustomed to the cold morning breeze coming through our window.

"Sof come on, it's too early for this," I say as she moves my phone from side to side.

She disregards my words and her jocular nature gets rid of any tiredness she felt. "You can have it back after you guess what I did last night," she says.

I cross my arms over my braless chest. "You slept?"

"Nope, you got one more guess, use it wisely." She keeps my phone in the air almost touching the dusty ceiling fan.

"You snored?" I snarl.

"No I sneaked out and talked to crepe guy, and I don't snore," she argues. She hands me back my phone and bites down on her bottom lip as she waits for my response. So this explains the loud noise I heard during the middle of the night, I kind of thought I was going crazy.

"For one, you do snore," I say getting that out of the way first. "Two, why the hell did you go out and see him?"

Sofia does a little shrug. "Because I wanted to have a formal introduction with him, he's really nice Candace, like really nice, and I swear there's nothing wrong with him."

For some reason my cheeks begin to grow hot and as much as I try to do so I can't hide my smile. "He is?" I ask beginning to get more curious about this crepe guy.

"Mhmm the nicest and the sweetest, now come on I need something to eat." Sofia lets me stand by my bed with a smile for a second before we both begin getting ready for the day. Of course Sofia takes the longest as she goes through every makeup item in her sparkling red purse. I just threw on some jeans and a sweater while Sofia is wearing a whole chartreuse dress with her hair up in a high bun. All I did with my hair was simply brush it and as for my face all I did was put on a simple coat of cherry Chap Stick that makes me eager to have breakfast.

"Okay, all ready, lets grub," Sofia announces once she has golden hoops hanging from her ears.

"Took you long enough," I mumble, but don't waste time in heading towards the door. Along with her meal card and mini purse Sofia grabs her camera and presses the on button.

"A beautiful Thursday on campus, let's go," she shouts.

We walk around campus where Sofia finds other people to film besides me, and when we get to the cafeteria we settle on bowls of cheerios at a table in the middle of all the bustling students wearing sweats and tired visages.

Sofia places her camera not too far from us, and between scoops she smiles at the camera.

"I thought you only filmed when you have an assignment," I ask trying to hide behind the thick layers of my hair.

"Well I want to film every life moment now, to really capture my college experience."

"Can't you just capture the exciting or important ones, not us shoving cereal in our faces," I argue. Seriously, I don't want any footage of milk coming down my chin showing up on my timeline in the next few years.

Sofia gestures to our bowls that are almost empty. "Shoving cereal in our faces is something to remember when we grow old and can't have sugar early in the morning." Sofia puts another bite in her mouth and waves to her camera.

We spend some more minutes eating before we make our way out of the cafeteria. On our way out we pass the many stations and of course Sofia's eyes widen as we get some feet away from the crepe station.

I can't even get a good look at the dusty station before Sofia faces me, blocking my view. "There he is!" she shouts but her high bun only lets me see the beaming lights that falls on the crepe toppings.

"Let me see," I whisper as there is a table of people from the school newspaper close by.

Sofia doesn't budge and instead pulls a makeup brush out of her mini bag after handing me her camera. Knowing how persistent Sofia is I don't even try to move away as she begins dabbing pink blush on my cheeks. She puts the brush back in her bag and strokes some hair out of my face as I give her back her camera that she didn't bother turning off.

"Go get 'em girl," she says.

"What? I'm not going over there?" I say and try to look past her hair towards the station.

"Candace, you know I don't like those two words, 'I'm not', now face those fears and smile for the camera." She puts the camera in my face and I cover my eyes with my arm. I'm about to act like a stubborn child and just stay in the same place with a pout, but I spot Sarah walking my way with a group of track girls, and my cheeks begin to burn up as I start walking.

"The plain Jane crepe doesn't taste so bad, just drown it with honey," Sofia shouts as I get closer to the station. *At least I have some extra money in my pocket.* As I approach the line and feel all of the lights in the cafeteria on me I ignore all of the students walking around with textbooks or good food and come into my thoughts. *Come on Candace, you're 18, you used to talk to all the boys in cross country, why is this making you so nervous? You're Candace Palmer, 4 medals, 5 first place wins. You got this.*

As the one boy with dreadlocks down to his back moves from the cash register I quicken my pace.

"Next," the same husky voice from yesterday says.

Looking right at me with piercing blue eyes and a warm smile that probably melts the crepe chocolate is a guy who is not what I expected in any of the conversations I had with Sofia. I have to give her credit, this guy is making me want to order these crepes.

"Hi," I say softly, trying not to look at the powerful blue of his eyes. My heart begins to beat uncontrollably like I'm on the track and I focus my eyes on my clear fingernails.

"Hey what can I get you today," the guy says making me look up at him. His warm smile still remains and he adjusts the brown snapback on his head that says *Fanny's Crepes* in the same bright orange font. It looked a little tacky on the middle aged woman I saw scooping bananas, but on him it looks good.

Before I muster up the words to speak my eyes catch sight of the white name tag hanging from his yellow shirt. Noah, it reads and I say it in a smooth spoken person's voice in my head.

"Umm I'll have a plain Jane crepe with a lot of honey," I say with a nod. Thinking of the crepe taste from yesterday I add, "A lot of honey."

Noah lets out a slight laugh, and types in something in the register. "You're really brave," he says as I hand him a crumbled $5 bill. I think he's talking about me coming up to such a cute guy like him, but then I remember it takes a brave man to eat what I'm about to eat and I laugh. I don't try to alter my laugh and laugh my normal laugh which luckily doesn't include a snort.

He laughs as well and begins preparing the crepe with clear plastic gloves. I watch every move he makes until he brings me the crepe on what I notice are two paper plates.

I notice there's no honey on my crepe and I'm about to ask, but he places a jar of honey shaped like a bear next to my crepe on the counter.

"I'll let you decide how much you're going to need," Noah says.

"Thanks."

I take the bottle and squeeze a heart on the crepe with Noah's eyes glued to me.

"Nice," he says nodding.

"I try my best," I say before picking up my plate.

"Good luck," are Noah's last words to me before we lock eyes for a millisecond.

"I'll need it."

I take one last look at the gorgeous warm smile on his face and let another giggle escape my lips.

When I get to Sofia whose arm is tired from holding her camera I say, "We're only eating crepes from now on."

# Chapter 4

The fall sun treats us runners on the track like bacon on a skillet with too much olive oil. Most of the boys on the team have abandoned their shirts, and me and the other girls are dressed in sports bras and spandex shorts.

"I know it's hot, but that doesn't mean we're going to stop hustling," Coach yells from the middle of the field. Today he's holding two huge gray water bottles as opposed to his usual one with lemon. Still with his gallons of water that now have slices of lime in them his dark complexion is glossed with sweat, as he watches us around the track. Today we're doing 4 200 meter sprints which seems less tiring than the miles we did yesterday, but after doing one and not being able to take a long break in between it gets exhausting.

"Next group," Coach yells just as I get comfortable standing on the prickling turf. I take my place at lane 8 with my eyes straight ahead. I'm about to go into my mode of deep concentration seeing coach raise his whistle to his lips, but he lowers it and starts yelling instead. "Sarah there's still an extra lane, go with them!" he shouts and even though we're pretty far away everyone within 5 feet of the track can hear him.

Breaking my intense stare with the track in front of me I look over at the turf where Sofia stands in line with her hands on her hips. "You've got to be kidding me," Sarah mumbles and throws her head back. She takes her place right in the lane next to me and she flashes a smirk my way before we both look ahead along with the other girls in our group.

The chirping birds in the sky, the cheerleaders in the bleachers, and all of the many distractions go away the second coach exhales and blows his whistle. It takes no time for me to begin darting down the track consumed in my thoughts. *You got this Candace, come on, she's tired, and she's already tomato truck red.* For a second I get out of my own head and look to my side to see the other three girls are behind me and Sarah and I are neck and neck. *Push Candace, push Candace, come on, one more 100 meter.* This is only my second 200, but I'm sprinting like the track is made of lava, and I'm not the only one. Sarah seems to be going at the same pace.

We stay like this and no matter how much energy I put into it, we're still right beside each other. I have longer legs so I guess I beat her by the tip of my shoe, but that's not enough for me.

"Good job," Sarah says showing off that she can speak while still catching her breath.

"Thanks you too," I mumble. As the rest of the girls get to the orange cone Coach placed to mark 200 meters, coach blows his whistle for the next group and I make my way over to the starting line repeating various mantras in my head. *Next time Candace, next time Candace, hard work pays off, you were so close, so damn close.* I repeat this in my head as I march through the bright green turf. The amount of time I repeat the two words, "next time," don't seem to matter, and the next sprints I do Sarah doesn't leave my side.

To make the feeling of being slow worse, coach gathers us all around him the second we're about to exit through the silver fence.

"Come on this will only take a few minutes then you can go back to whatever it is that keeps all of you so energized," Coach says as we cluster into a group. Something a bunch of sweaty people who just ran for 40 minutes should not be doing especially in this afternoon heat. Frankly I'm not too sure why we're this close when there's a whole football field encompassing us. Still we all manage to focus our attention on Coach which is pretty easy since he's 6 feet 4.

"Anyway as most of you know we have a track meet coming up in a few weeks, and it will be hosted on our campus." Some people slap their foreheads, but I've already known about this track meet for a few weeks due to the color coded calendar I share with Sofia. "As I was saying all of you know what section you'll be running in. If you don't, please come see me. This track meet is really important so I need all of you on your A game." Coach stops and looks each of us in our eyes. "No late night ramen noodles funny business, now go on to get some rest." We all scatter to the fences, but the Coach's eyes narrow on me and before I can take another step he shouts, "Candace not so fast."

I was so close! I go over to coach and force a smile on my face as he takes a large gulp from his water bottle. When a good portion of the water is gone he begins to speak. "Your mile has decreased drastically, and I want you to run the mile along with the 200, you think you're up for it?" I don't even think about it before I begin to nod. A mile and a 150 meter is nothing; especially since track meets are hours long and there is usually so much time between each event.

"I'm completely up for it, but are you sure my mile is fast enough?"

"What do I tell you kids? It's not about being fast, you've improved Candace and you work hard." Coach turns to his side and lets out a sigh. "But if you want to do better, maybe you should tell your friend to stop filming me."

I look over to where coach's eyes are and behind the fence Sofia stands not blending in with any of the athletes as she wears a striped jumpsuit and holds her camera.

"Sorry she's a film student," I mumble, but Coach's scold doesn't disappear.

"I'm not Chadwick Bozeman stop filming me!" He shouts and heads to the opposite end of the track.

"Wow that was a great shot, do you think he can do it again?" Sofia asks. I can't tell if she's serious as her expression is hiding behind her camera, but I shake my head before grabbing my gym bag and walking beside Sofia. We look like complete opposites with my messy black flyaways and Sofia's curls that give off a strong coconut smell. When Sofia has captured the brown and amber leaves sprouting from the trees she finally turns her camera off, making it the first time in a week that I've seen the silver object without a flashing green dot.

"Time for crepes," she squeaks as we walk down campus where we step on crackling leaves.

For the past week or so ever since I ordered that plain Jane crepe Sofia and I have found ourselves going to the cafeteria just to share a crepe drowned in sweetener to mask the taste. I've suffered one stomach ache, probably gained some weight, but as cheesy as it sounds it's pretty much worth it when I swallow and see Noah's smile behind the plastic window scooping berries.

"We can't get crepes now I need to change first," I say gesturing to my small shorts and sports bra combination.

"Fine but if you ask me you look great," Sofia says. She begins sashaying in the direction of our dorm, but she stops when she's five feet ahead of me. "But you could use a brush."

It's almost as if going to get a crepe is one of my top priorities in college. Where did I go wrong? Sofia and I waste no time getting to our dorm. Of course when I change into some jeans and a shirt Sofia can't resist applying more eyeliner on herself and almost persuading me to put some on. We look in the mirror and change several things about our hair before we finally head down to the cafeteria. I stop in my tracks when we reach the glass double doors and take a small look at everyone inside.

I turn to Sofia. "Why are we doing this? I mean what's the point in eating crap for a guy I hardly know," I argue. "We barely even talked when I order and I have a track meet coming up, why is this guy making me do this? "

Sofia exchanges looks between the glass doors and me. "Come on you blush every time you see him, plus this is just stage one, it only gets more interesting from here." She bats her eyelashes and I stop looking at the hungry students behind the glass doors and instead look at my reflection. I pull some strands behind my eyes before Sofia turns her camera back on, and we walk through the crowded cafeteria where dinner has just begun being served.

Before heading to the back of the cafeteria Sofia and I wait in line for some salads that are 95% lettuce and 5% croutons and dressing. The cafeteria is so crowded we don't bother sitting at a table close to the crepe station and squish at a table where Sofia's student council friends are. Sofia isn't really close with them and we sit on the sides of the table stabbing at our salads while her "friends," gossip and complain about everything there is to complain about.

A girl with a red streak through her black hair groans, "Ugh did you see Aurora's beige couch? its way better than mine," she whines. They go on complaining and complaining and when Sofia and I have picked out the good stuff from our salads we get up and make our way to the crepe station.

We're right on time when we choose to start walking as the middle aged woman is no longer at the cash register and Noah glows while tapping his fingers against the probably empty cash register.

Unlike all the other times I've approached the register I'm not too flustered, but there still remains a tightness in my stomach that doesn't feel all too bad as I glue my eyes on Noah. Sofia doesn't even have to convince me a billion times and she just finds her place at a table where she and her camera have a perfect view of me.

"Well if it isn't my favorite customer," Noah beams when I approach the marble counter where a tip jar sits.

"If it isn't my favorite server," I respond. I stand right in front of him looking into his deep blue eyes not being able to hold back my smile.

Noah adjusts his hat. "Oh come on, I know the guy at the taco stand tells better jokes," he laughs. *Well the taco stand guy isn't as cute as you.* If I was Sofia I would probably say that, but I'm not and I just continue blushing until Noah's smooth voice catches my attention. "So same order of torture?" He asks.

"You know me so well." Gosh I need to work on my conversation skills.

"Well I wasn't kidding when I said you're my favorite customer." It might just be the bright lights but I'm pretty sure his eyes are becoming bluer.

For some reason I lose the ability to censor my thoughts and say, "Are there really so many to choose from?" I say looking around the empty tables and seats. I smirk to mask the blow of my comment and fortunately Noah lets out the smoothest laugh.

"Wow," he says not losing his smile. He lowers his tone and leans in a little more making it feel like we're in our own little bubble. "Look if I could make these crepes better and have everyone in this cafeteria come here I would, but you'd still be my favorite customer." He smiles for a moment and then lets my name play on the tip of his tongue. I'm at a loss for words until I remember Noah and I aren't in our little bubble and still in the back of our cafeteria.

"I'm happy to be your favorite customer."

After our little exchange I take my plain Jane crepe with several grains of salt and honey. I head back over to the table where Sofia is filming and she puts her camera down to smile from cheek to cheek. "How did it go?" She shouts more than asks.

"Great."

I smile to myself and remembering Noah's words actually gets me through the thick bites of the crepe. Sofia throws a bunch of questions at me and I give her all the answers she wants even though it's just regarding a 5 minute conversation maybe less.

When I'm done with my crepe and have put the honey coated plate in the trash Sofia takes me by surprise and grabs my arm. In a matter of seconds, we're back at the crepe counter and Noah's blue eyes are staring back at me making me completely flustered.

Luckily I don't have to speak as Sofia begins talking. "Hi Noah," she says.

"Hey girl who can't stop filing people," he jokes. He looks from me to Sofia and I can't stop admiring his features from his impeccable jawline to the dimples that don't disappear as he keeps on smiling. *Gosh this guy is making me soft.*

Sofia wastes no time and blurts out, "So Noah, what do you think of my dear friend Candace?" Oh my gosh, did she really just say those words.

I can't decide if I should look at Noah or scold Sofia, but my eyes land on Noah as he begins to speak. "I think your friend Candace is someone I want to get to know more." His voice is so smooth. I want to hear more, but he doesn't continue speaking and my heart begins to beat all too fast as if I just finished a mile. He doesn't continue to talk and grabs a small slip of paper on the counter and begins scribbling something on it with a black pen. He picks up the slip of paper and hands it to me. "I would exchange numbers using my phone like a normal person in 2019, but I'm working so this is the best I can do."

I take the slip of paper and smile at the series of numbers written in perfect handwriting.

"Thank you," is all I'm able to say before Sofia shrieks and puts her camera in my face. Sofia and I aren't even out of the cafeteria before I aggressively type the number into my contacts. Due to Sofia's advice it isn't until after my track practice that I actually go to Noah's contact, and begin typing while lying on my bed. *Me: Hey, hopefully this isn't the wrong number and some serial killer, oh this is Candace by the way.* I quickly delete that text and begin typing a new text that hopefully won't make me sound like a weirdo. *Me. Hey, it's Candace, I'm the one who orders the plain Jane.* I send it and seconds later my phone buzzes with a text message from Noah. *Noah: All you had to say was it's my favorite customer.*

# Chapter 5

"And because the shielding in an atom and the distance stays the same as you go across a period, the coulombic force increases," Professor Springman says in his monotone voice. He stands at the bottom of the lecture hall pacing slowly and pushing up his silver glasses every 5 seconds not keeping me or the rest of the student's attention. At this point we're all just subconsciously writing down or typing notes waiting to digest them in a late night cram session.

"I'm never going to even use chemistry, I want to own a t t-shirt brand," the boy next to me mumbles. I don't respond and try not to notice he's been watching some YouTube videos with his air pods. He better not ask me for notes at the end, unless he plans to pay me.

Professor Springman is about to continue but the bell blares through the whole wide room waking up some students who were nodding off with their mouths open.

"Well that's it for today I'd tell you about the test, but none of you seem to be listening," he mumbles before picking up his coffee cup and taking a large sip. He definitely needs some caffeine, I sit pretty far away in the lecture hall, but those eye bags of

Mr. Springman's are as huge as the hearts the girl in front of me has been drawing on her paper. Her doodling habit reminds me of Noah who I've been texting ever since he gave me his number, and I've learned he's pretty funny and my fingers have gone numb several times when my eyes were on his contact. I've probably texted him more than I have texted my mother who is still having trouble learning to use her iPhone.

I scatter out of the lecture hall with the rest of the assemblage of students who look relieved not to be learning about how many valence electrons are in a hydrogen atom. I walk out of the science building swiftly holding my messenger bag and admiring the bright sun that is way more effulgent when I'm not running around the track. As chemistry 101 was my last class of the day I begin making my way to my dorm, but I stop when I feel my phone vibrate against my jean pocket.

"Hey, watch it!" A passing girl on a bike yells the second I pull my phone out and stop in the middle of the pathway.

"Sorry," I mumble. She should've said "I'm on your right," but I don't care as I move away from the pathway and find my place against a tree. I expect to get a text from Noah saying something like good afternoon plain Jane which is his nickname for me now, but instead Sofia's contact appears on my screen. This has to be the first time I'm not completely excited to hear from Sofia. I look at my screen and knit my brows at Sofia's message. *Sofia: Don't come to the dorm, meet me at the campus cafe ASAP.* Just as I'm about to question why Sofia is in the too cold campus cafe that tries to be like Starbucks, and is right across from the campus cafeteria, Sofia texts me again. Sofia: *Don't even hesitate, come on I ordered you that green tea latte you like so much.* Right under the blue bubble of that text she sends a photo of a plastic cup filled with my favorite green liquid. In thick black ink Sofia's name is scribbled beside the notorious California logo. My fingers tap my keyboard vigorously and I text her *on my way.*

"Watch out!" Another girl on a light blue cruiser screams right as I step onto the pathway.

"Sorry," I mumble and jet across the pathway in the direction of the campus cafe. Hidden behind big trees along the crimson pathway that leads to the campus cafeteria is the campus cafe which is kind of a waste of space because the campus cafeteria serves coffee and better warm pastries. My feet want to go in the direction of the cafeteria and see Noah smiling in the dusty area of the cafeteria, but I head to the cafe where the big see through windows are being hit by the komorebi. I walk into the cafe and Sofia's big blossoming curls are the first thing I see tucked away in a booth beside the wall. I begin walking in the cold cafe towards her, but in 5 steps I see her and the two medium sized drinks aren't alone. Across from her in the same shaky stool sits a guy dressed in all black with hair filled with too much gel. It may be the leather jacket, or his devious smirk, but there is something stygian about him or rather familiar, but I don't let this Taylor Lautner impersonator stop me from tapping on Sofia's shoulder.

"Ooh there you are! I've been waiting for you," Sofia says and wraps her arms around me.

I know this is not a real hug, and Sofia proves it as she begins to whisper in my ear, "Be nice, I was talking about you, and he said he wanted to meet you."

"K," I respond masking my confusion. She unravels her arms and I sit on the stool between her and the guy whose smirk is now directed at me.

"Candace this is Brayden he's in one of my film classes, Brayden this is Candace my roommate and inspiration." Sofia gestures to her camera that I didn't notice is sitting on the rim of the window, of course with the green light on.

Brayden nods and holds out his hand. "Nice to meet you Candace," he says. I shake his cold hand and as I look into his dark eyes I feel like I've seen him somewhere before. Was he on an episode of twilight? Or maybe he's that guy from that car insurance commercial. I shake the thought off and take a sip of my green tea latte. I expect Sofia and Brayden to continue whatever they were talking about, but Brayden's eyes still haven't left me.

"You're on the track team right?" he asks and his raspy voice makes me barely catch his words. I stop sipping my drink and look from Sofia's smile to Brayden's smirk.

"Yeah," I say. I look at Sofia's widening eyes for some telepathic message and after some seconds of not talking I get the message she wants me to go. Then again this message is only coming from her arched eyebrows and the way her and Brayden are exchanging looks. I look between them one more time before I grab the last bit of my green tea latte and say, "Well I should go I have to," I stutter as I try to make an excuse. Like god knows I need an excuse; I look over at the cafeteria and my mind goes instantly to Noah. "I'm going to ask Noah out," I blurt out, not too sure of my thoughts. *Really Candace the only things you know about this guy are his food likes and dislikes. He likes avocados, dislikes olives, and has never tried pumpkin pie.*

I'm not sure if I'm going to pursue the words I just said, but Sofia's face lights up while Brayden begins to scroll through his phone. "Aww you are," she says covering her mouth. Getting Brayden to look up from his phone she whispers, "Noah is her lover, they're going to have a little dalliance someday?" Brayden raises his eyebrows and doesn't let go of his phone.

"Dalliance?" he says exactly what I'm thinking.

Just as Sofia is about to explain the word dalliance, I throw away my empty cup and give Sofia a half hug. For a second she looks up at me and as she looks at me I see a different message than the one I thought I received, but her gaze immediately goes away when she turns back to Brayden who I believe is playing footsie with her under the small round table.

"Tell me about it," Sof yells when I exit the cafe.

I can't give her a response because my mind is filled with too many thoughts as I simultaneously stroke some of the flyways behind my ears. *You're not nervous Candace, come on you've run two miles on just a chocolate chip protein bar, and if you want to ask out Noah you can do that. Wait*

*Candace you're not running or about to beat someone up, why are you talking yourself up so much?*

I get out of my head and push the door to the campus cafeteria letting a brief breeze hit my face and move all the flyaways I just slicked back. Since I've come in from the back entrance I don't have time to walk through the many people in the cafeteria and the first station I see is the only one I've cared about these last few weeks. The gross crepe station, where the only thing sweet is Noah. *Gosh I sound so stupid.*

I go up to the crepe counter where the other middle aged woman stands behind the cashier. I'm pretty sure she and Noah are the only two employees who work at the vacant station.

"Oh it's you again," the woman with dowdy brown hair says. She adjusts her brown cap and narrows her eyes at me.

My words fall out of my mouth and I can't control them. "Hi I was wondering if Noah is here, I'm Candace he said I'm his favorite customer, but that's not the point, my friend says we kind of have a dalliance," at these words I stop rambling like some stupid girl.

The woman whose name tag reads Mabel finds my babbling risible and shakes her head from side to side. "Ahh young love I remember when I was an ingénue," she says looking up at the ceiling. She stays this way for a few seconds until she comes back to reality and looks at me. "Oh right, Noah's sitting just over there. The lucky duck doesn't have a shift today."

"Thanks." I turn around and seeing Noah not in his uniform but in a graphic tee that captivates me along with his blue eyes that look chartreuse with the cafeteria lighting. I make my way over to him as he sits comfortably at a table alone writing on some paper.

"Candace I was wondering when I would see you again," Noah says immediately when I reach the table he is at. He gestures for me to sit and I sit across from him looking into his eyes hoping he doesn't see how tremulous I am.

"You were?" I ask.

He flashes that award winning smile. "Texting you is fun, but seeing you is always better."

"Likewise," I say practically bubbling on the inside.

"Likewise you sound like my English teacher in 9th grade."

"Well what else was I supposed to say?"

"Uhh, I don't know maybe Noah wow you look great when you're not working in that uniform of yours."

"Well, I wanted to let you know seeing you is better than texting." And I mean that.

"So you're saying I'm not a good texter? Are you saying I ain't too good with words or something?" Noah plays around with his eyebrows.

"I'm saying whatever you want to hear." Well that sounded more flirtatious and amatory than I expected. Still my somewhat bold and a little too submissive statement doesn't pop the bubble Noah and I are in as he refuses to take his eyes off of me.

He finally drops the pen he's been playing with and somehow his sculpted face lights up some more. "If you're saying what I want to hear than I guess you must be about to ask me out?" He says smoothly as if he isn't reading my mind and reminding me of what I set out to do when coming inside the cafeteria. Sure Noah's eyes make me want to beg to go out with him, but I decide to take a page out of Sofia's book. "Well I was actually going to ask the taco cart guy." Who actually is an 80 year old man, but Noah lets out a laugh achieving my goal.

"Before you ask Mr. Cortez who I believe has to go to his granddaughter's quinceanera, maybe you should consider what I have to offer." I like where this is headed.

"And what offer is that?" I am really getting good at this whole playful conversation thing, but I have to thank Noah for that because he's so easy to talk to, unlike Mr. Cortez who has a very strong mean mug.

Noah leans in a little more. "Saturday night I pick you up at 7, and we'll take it from there," he says softly.

I give up my whole cool girl act and immediately begin to nod. "I would love that."

"Great well I have to go, but it's a date then." Noah grabs the pen and binder from the table and we both get up. As he stands I can't help, but notice his white Adidas sneaker that doesn't have a scrape on them unlike mine. My eyes wander to look at his other shoe, but there is none and in its place is a prosthetic. *How come I didn't know this about him?*

Realizing I've been looking at his shoe and what I thought was a shoe for a little too long I look back into his eyes.

"I'll see you around," I say abruptly.

"Hopefully," he responds and flashes me another smile.

We exchange goodbyes and I head out of the cafeteria to be greeted by the sight of Sofia walking out of the cafe holding her camera and looking at Brayden. I swear I know him from somewhere, but I forget about that thought and instead think about Noah and the fact he doesn't have two legs which I guess I just expected from everyone I've met so far.

# Chapter 6

The week went by fast and it's now Saturday morning with clouds that are conflating and wind that's blowing the palm trees left and right. I stand on the starting line of the track not accompanied by my teammates or coach just me and the janitors cleaning the bleachers. I don't have Coach's whistle to yell at me to go, and instead the voice in my head is more calming and pushing me through this solo weekend workout. *Go Candace.* I tell myself, and begin running down the track with the help of my workout playlist. I can't use my workout playlist during regular practice because Coach doesn't believe listening to music actually improves physical performance. I could show him all of the many statistics from every notable magazine, but he would still yell, "No listening to Kendrick Lamar! If you want motivation make up your own lyrics." I guess I use this advice because in a way I'm listening to my own lyrics or thoughts as I try to get this mile in 5 minutes. Come on Candace, almost finished with this lap, 3 more to go then you can go to your dorm and take a nice long nap. And then guess what? Soon after that you'll be going to the mysterious place Noah won't tell me about, and you'll be holding hands and hopefully doing more. At that thought of having my date tonight I quicken my pace and finish my first lap continuing to think of all the places Noah could possibly take me.

What if he just takes me to the cafeteria? No he wouldn't do that he's too much of a gentleman. *Well at least he seems like a gentleman. Maybe we will go bowling or do something like horseback riding. Chill Candace I think a guy has to know a girl for more than three months before taking her to ride an animal. Wait can he ride an animal with, you know, one leg?*

I shake the thought out of my head and finish my second lap. I can't pretend I haven't been thinking about Noah being an amputee even though I feel like some vain piece of crap stressing over some superficial detail. I've never met someone or had a talk with someone who had lost one of their limbs, but before college I hadn't met a lot of people. Innocent, just out of high school, Candace hadn't met any potheads, people who only sleep 4 hours, or girls like Sofia who have watched Pretty Woman more than 15 times. All that changed within a month, so maybe I need to stop being so narrow minded. Noah is too good of a person for me to be vain.

These thoughts about Noah are so distracting, I finish my mile without noticing. Even though my legs feel like I ran my hardest, I'm still seconds off from the low time I want to be at.

I leave the track and walk to my dorm taking advantage of each step getting my breath back. Feeling a harsh stomach growl erupt in my torso I buy two warm croissants from a coffee stand along the lawn outside of my dorm. Sure I could get a crepe, but if I really want to start my day off right I'm going to need something I won't have to drown in sugar.

"Honey I'm home," I shout as I push my dorm door open.

"No one cares," a passing student with the largest eye bags says.

"Some people should really sleep in more," I mumble and walk into my dorm.

I'm about to present the croissant to Sophia, but I stop in my tracks when I see her sitting on the floor cross legged smiling at Brayden. Brayden has his usual devious smirk and dark clothing that contrast with the bright colors on Sophia's side of the room. Brayden's not sitting on the floor, but spinning a little in my desk chair like he's the one who bought the purple piece of furniture from Target.

"Sophia's inspiration, nice to see you again," Brayden says and one of his eyebrows bounces up.

"Nice to see you too," I lie and Sophia's face lights up at the sight of the buttery croissant in my hand.

"Aww aren't you the best," she squeals. I hand her the pastry. I'm still weirded out by Brayden's presence because this dorm, much like all the others is only made for two people.

"Brayden was helping me edit some footage while I educate him on American snacks." Sofia gestures to the assortment of salty snacks that are scattered on the carpet. As I sit on my bed Sofia leans in and whispers, "He's Canadian."

I nod and sit on my bed still looking at Brayden who has now spun around in the desk chair and is typing on IMovie. How Sofia is educating him on all the salty snacks when Brayden's back is turned, I don't know, but him focusing on Sofia's laptop gives Sofia the chance to turn and begin talking to me.

"So how was the morning run? Are you finally tired of running for a number on a stopwatch?" she asks.

I shake my head. "Of course not, I'm just excited for my date with Noah." I say this with a straight face, but Sofia's is the complete opposite. "I can't believe Candace Palmer is going on her first date!" she says too loud.

"It's not my first date," I Immediately argue and take my last bite of croissant.

Brayden spins around in my chair and looks at us while his smirk grows. "This is your first date?" he asks like it's his business. I'm not even listening to his comment and trying to find any trace of a Canadian accent in his voice.

Looking at my leggings and watching Sofia's eyes stab into my soul, I say, "It's not my first date, remember I told you about Brian Wilkers in the 10th grade." After taking a bite of her croissant Sofia covers her mouth in an attempt to not let her laughter escape. Let's just say it was a failed attempt.

"The boy who you said smelled like onions and ate the last slice of the pizza you guys were sharing." Sofia engrosses herself in her croissant, but still shoots me a look making me remember the actual date I went on 4 years ago.

Thinking of the awful date where I watched a boy shove pizza in his face I keep on arguing. "Still it doesn't matter if it was a bad date, it counts as my first." I finish my croissant and don't see Sofia's expression when my back is turned as I throw away my napkin. I flop back on my bed and my eyes land on Brayden who is looking at Sofia as she moves her cross legged position to laying on the carpet giving Brayden a view of what her velvet pink shorts are displaying. *Creep.*

Sofia isn't even aware of his eyes and she's instead finishing her croissant before handing one of the snacks to Brayden. The snacks she used to keep under her bed and share with me.

Wanting to have a good talk with my best friend without any testosterone present I look in Brayden's direction, and say to Sofia, "Sof don't you think Brayden is working exceptionally hard and could use a break."

Sofia plays with some of the candy wrappers and looks from me to Brayden. Of course it takes her a bit to get the hint. "Oh yeah Brayden we can do this again tomorrow," she says. She jumps up from the ground and wraps her arms around Brayden when he finally gets off of my chair. As they hug Brayden's hand gets close to gracing Sofia's butt, but I shoot him a death stare making them exchange goodbyes before Brayden finally leaves.

When the door is shut Sofia goes back to sitting on the floor and I let my curiosity get the best of me. "So what's going on with you two?" I ask.

Sofia bites down on her glossy pink lips. "You saw, he's my editing buddy." Her words are full of quiescence and I can't accept them. *Hmm editing buddy who you let eat all of your good snacks?*

It's like Sofia is reading my mind thus making her change the subject. "Enough talking about me I'm boring, do you know what you're going to wear on your date tonight?"

"I don't know he hasn't told me where we're going he says it's a surprise."

Sofia's eyes widened. "Oooh a surprise, maybe he's gonna take you to meet his parents, he looks like a guy who would do that."

"Oh does he?"

"Yes and speaking of the elephant in the room, I don't think it's a big deal."

"Oh, yeah it's totally not a big deal," I say and for some reason my face starts getting all hot.

Sofia slits her eyes. "Do I sense some uncertainty?"

I don't hesitate to shake my head. "No, if I was unsure it would mean I'm vain, and that the amount of limbs on a person matters to me."

Sofia continues to narrow her eyes without saying a word. This is something she only does when she wants an answer or is about to burp.

Seeing she's not going to stop I begin babbling. "Don't you think it will be weird because I'm a runner, and spend most of my time using my legs?"

"I'm not going to lie, that's what I was thinking, but you know opposites attract." Her voice gets all high pitched. "But what if he's just a smidge taller than you, and you wanna do that thing where you step on his shoes for a kiss." *Is this really what she's thinking about?*

"I haven't thought about that Sof."

"Well when it comes to the running thing just don't tell him you're an aspiring track star, it will probably make him feel weird anyway."

"Sof, I can't lie to him. If anything that would just make things weirder."

She does a small shrug. "It won't be a lie, just a tiny secret."

"Sofia it's not a tiny secret; track is my whole life and I have a meet coming up."

"You do! Ooh cool I love the food at those, those hot dogs are the best."

Sofia and I stop talking about Noah and instead go into a full tangent about the best track meet food. We don't stop talking about if popcorn is better with or without salt until my phone buzzes with Noah's name across my screensaver. Immediately all my worries go away seeing his name.

*Noah: I hate to sound demanding, but wear something fancy.*

Sofia sees my excitement and it transfers onto her face and in her eyes. "It's him isn't it?" She sticks out her hand.

Reluctantly I hand her the phone.

Sofia lowers her voice into her English Dutch accent. "Ooh 'I don't mean to sound demanding,' isn't he the nicest."

I laugh at her comment letting out some of the giddiness that is bottled up inside me.

Screw Brian Wilkers and the pizza parlor we went to, this is going to be my first date and it's going to be amazing.

For a good portion of our day Sofia and I chill in the dorm enjoying our Saturday and watching some Friday Night Lights re-runs, We don't end our indulgent chilling session until my alarm goes off telling me it's five and socially acceptable to get ready for my date.

Sofia brings out her whole makeup kit and practically puts a dent in her mattress when she plops it in the center. She knows I don't do the whole full face of makeup thing, but she still instructs me to sit in my spinning chair.

She digs through all of her brushes, powders, and concealers. "We don't even know what I'm going to wear," I whine as Sofia grabs some tubes that only have product clinging to the inside. Sofia begins dabbing stuff on my face as she talks. "Oh, yeah we do, where have you been?"

My eyes are closed, but I can tell in her tone she has that cocky expression on her face. "Uhh I've been stressing about finding something fancy in my closet." I feel something being rubbed on my cheekbone, and my first reaction is to flinch, but the cool bristles or what I think are bristles bring a nice cool feeling to my skin.

"Well you won't need to do that anymore I found a perfect dress for you in mine, we might have shoved all of those crepes in our mouths, but we're still the same size." Hearing Sofia's words that are awfully close to my face I go against her orders and open my eyes.

"Aww you're going to give me one of your dresses?" She has several beautiful dresses she never even wears herself so it's not that big of a deal, but it's still nice to know she's going to let me wear one instead of selling them on some online store. I'm not that into dresses, but if I'm going to wear one I'd rather it be from Sofia's closet than anyone else's.

"Yes I am, but don't get too excited, I'm going to need it back." She has one of those weird shaped pink things in her hand, she says, "close your eyes," like my mom or one of those ladies who work at Sephora. We spend every minute up until 6:45 getting me ready for the date while listening to Sofia's music that blares from her iPhone speaker. It only takes 3 songs for Sofia to fit me in one of her dresses and for me to disappoint her a little by tying my hair back in a ponytail. What can I say? She put me in a dress, so I get to not have my hair flying everywhere no matter how aesthetically unpleasing it looks. Frankly I don't care about how I look, and I prove this when I'm slouching on my bed awakened by a knock on the door. Sofia jumps up from my shoulder and pulls me off the bed only for her to instruct me to walk slowly on our soft carpet. I can't keep the cool girl act up any longer as I bite down on my bottom lip and swing the door open. I'm graced by the sight of Noah in a black blazer looking flawless.

"Hey," he says, making me forget about all the prep that went into my look. Like always, I fail at trying to hold back my smile.

# Chapter 7

After leaving Sofia behind, who would have easily passed as a mom on prom night with her camera. I walk beside Noah out of my dorm building where the sky is changing from a light blue to a lavender.

"So are you still not going to tell me where we're going?" I ask.

Noah's smile remains and he shakes his head along with the light breeze. "No I think I'm going to let the suspense build up a little," he says.

I let out a fake sigh, "If you say so, but Mr., Cortez would tell me," I say.

Noah leads me through the parking lot. Looking in his eyes and being this close to him makes me forget about his slight limp.

We walk over to a light blue buggy and as Noah presses a button on his keys letting me know it's his I stop in my tracks and smile at the small vehicle.

"Aww you drive a buggy!"

"Unfortunately, it's a hand me down," Noah says tapping the top of the car that is some inches below us.

"Unfortunately? It's the cutest thing ever."

Before he can open any of the blue doors I turn to him and punch him lightly in the arm. "Blue buggy no punch backs." *Damn it Candace you're not supposed to punch your date.*

"Sorry," I mumble seconds after the punch is thrown.

Noah opens the door to the passenger seat. "You better apologize, you're only like the 5th person to do that today." I settle in the passenger seat of his car and Noah closes the door before getting in the driver's seat where he starts the car.

We drive out of the parking lot and I tap my fingers on my lap as the period of silence becomes too long.

"So why do I only see you in the cafeteria?' I ask.

Noah keeps his eyes on the road, but I can tell I have his attention, "Because you are crazy and for some reason you keep eating the industrial egg-paste crepes."

My eyes are now glued to him. "No I mean like... that was a bad question, I mean what do you like to do when you're not working?"

"Well I'm studying literature, and I read, what about you?"

There's a sudden pang in my chest as I remember Sofia's words about not telling him about me running track.

I play with the ends of my hair before saying, "I'm majoring in business and I spend most of my time with Sofia doing god knows what."

"God knows what sounds fun." Noah continues driving and I think of all the questions I should ask him about himself along with the questions that would get me answers on where we're going. It's too late for those though as Noah's car comes to a slow stop and I finally take my eyes off of Noah to look outside of my window where a bunch of shops are packed closely together. The one that catches my eye is the store that we're directly parked in front of which is a small pink building with a bright sign that says *le petit jours* in some exaggerated cursive.

The two large windows that are being lit by the inside lights give me a glimpse of a quint shape with spread out round tables.

Noah's voice makes me look away from the building. "I thought I would take you to get some actual quality crepes that are served by someone who is actually French." His words make me turn from the small cafe to his smooth smile.

"It was worth the surprise," I respond.

We get out of Noah's car walking side by side with our arms only inches away from each other. Like a gentleman, Noah didn't hesitate to open the see through door for me and my ballerina flats slapping against the clean white tiles of the cafe. The noise that erupted from my flats wasn't the same as the tapping noise from Noah's prosthetic which catches the attention of the lady hidden behind a cash register and a case of golden brown pastries. I notice the people by the window take glances at Noah, some subtle and others not, but their eyes and curiosity go away as we get closer to the lady.

The lady has the biggest smile on her face and looks between Noah and I. "Hi, how can I help you this evening," she says with the strongest French accent I've ever heard. I stand by Noah and I let him order for the both of us as I have no idea what to say.

After ordering some crepes with names I can't pronounce Noah chooses the perfect table in the cafe that gives us the view of the navy blue sky and the paintings of Paris on the walls. When we're sitting at our table face to face, my breathing speeds up and I can't exactly form words. I let my eyes wander across the cafe. Staring back at me is a little boy with circle glasses not looking at his macarons.

Getting my attention to transfer to him Noah says, "I think that boy might have a little crush on you."

I let out a small giggle. "You sure he just wasn't admiring the painting." I look at the painting of a Parisian street at night above us.

Noah places his hand on top of mine and instantly my nerves seem to settle at his touch. "No, trust me. He's looking at you, you're beautiful."

His jocular nature doesn't seem to be apparent and I believe each of his words as if I have never heard them before.

"Thank you you're too, I mean-" I stumble over my words.

Noah raises his eyebrows. "You mean?"

I try to form the right words, but I instead find the words that are just randomly floating in my head.

"I mean, you have a Leonardo DiCaprio charm." *Oh god Candace did you really just say that.*

There goes Noah's calming presence again making me release my fumbling mood-killer sentences.

With his hand not leaving mine he says, "Romeo and Juliet or The Great Gatsby?"

I bite down on my bottom lip and take a second to remember how much I loved Leonardo DiCaprio in each of those films.

"Both," I say. "More Romeo and Juliet though," I add.

Noah doesn't get a chance to respond when the lady with the strong French accent approaches our table with two trays that have the most enticing looking pastry on top of them. They definitely don't resemble what I have been eating in the cafeteria.

"Here you go," the lady says beaming at us. She takes extra care when placing Noah's plate on the table, but Noah doesn't hold one ounce of any unpleasant feeling in his deep blue eyes.

"So this is what crepes are supposed to look like," I say.

When the woman is done handing us the plates Noah removes his hand from on top of mine, but somehow the connection between us hasn't been altered.

Noah looks from his crepe to my smile when the woman struts back to the register. "Well don't get used to this. I still work at the campus, and the ingredients there aren't changing."

"Right, how did you get that job?"

Noah does a small shrug. "I realized I didn't want to be paying my student loans forever, so I found the job on one of the campus bulletins."

"Well do you like working there?"

Noah looks down at his shining fork. "I mean it's an alright job, but I met you there so of course I like it."

We begin eating our crepes and the taste doesn't compare to what Noah has been serving me in the cafeteria. The chocolate tastes like every single Lindour chocolate ball I've had on Valentine's Day, and it reminds me of all the pancakes I used to eat on Sunday mornings. I don't think I can go back to eating those cafeteria crepes ever again, but for Noah I'll settle.

When there's only chocolate syrup left on the edges of our plates I make sure there is no trace of what I just ate on my face.

"So how's track going?" he asks and for a moment I just blink in confusion.

We've been talking for some time and my words have just spilled out of me, but I swear I didn't say anything about my running due to Sofia's words this afternoon,

Having no idea what to say I can only answer the question Noah begins to ask. "I'm not a stalker, I've seen your photo on the school website."

I nod still in shock that he knows the information I was trying to restrict him from.

He leans in a little and his voice gets smooth. "Look Candace, I've been an amputee for about 10 years now, and something I learned is it takes nothing away from me that you're a female Usain Bolt."

I look down at my plate wishing there was still a crepe and I let out a soft almost inaudible "Sorry if I made things weird."

Noah reaches for my hand again and his touch even though I feel quite embarrassed decreases the thoughts jabbing myself for not being honest when he asked me what I spend my time doing.

"Don't be, you know how many times people have stopped running after passing me on a sidewalk? Some even stop doing the flamingo stretch when they get up from a lecture, which to be fair I can still kind of do."

"Well the flamingo isn't as fun, everyone knows cherry pickers are the best stretch." I smirk.

"Oh really?"

I nod and accidentally squeeze his hand a little tighter, though I'm not sure he noticed.

We talk for a little more before the woman from the register gives Noah the black leather check that he won't let me touch. I kind of wanted to have one of those moments where we both reach for the check, but I honestly probably couldn't pay for it with the crumbled $20 stashed away in the mini purse on my shoulder.

We exit the cafe, and instead of going back into Noah's car we walk down the Los Angeles streets that are being lit up by the glowing signs of restaurants with people going in and out of the various establishments.

"So you have two sisters?" I ask with my hand intertwined in Noah's.

"Yes they're older and they ruined Santa clause for me."

"Mine did too!"

"It sucks right, then your parents tell you-"

Finishing his thought I say, "Don't tell the kids in your class."

"It's because they get to have all the fun dreaming about a fat man breaking into their house."

Noah and I stop in front of an organic taco shop and we're facing each other under the detailed lights of the taco sign.

Once again I don't put thought into the words that are going to come out of my mouth, "Oh my bad, did I respond to what you said? I was going to say my dad is really skinny so I could obviously tell he wasn't Santa," I ramble.

Curing my nerves Noah pushes one of my thin flyaways behind my ear. "Don't worry about it," he whispers and gets closer to me.

I take a glimpse at his prosthetic just for the sake of looking but Noah lightly lifts my head up with just one of his fingers. He engulfs me in his cinnamon scent still lingering from the French place. He presses his lips against mine and his hands fall along my waist. I kiss him back as I burn up on the inside, and we don't stop embracing each other until someone on a bike comes rushing past us. This makes the flyaway Noah tucked in fly in front of my eyes, but I barely notice.

This has been way better than that stupid pizza parlor date. Our kiss in the middle of the street felt like a scene in a low budget hallmark movie. Afterwards, we head back to Noah's car. Unlike the drive to this place, we savor each mile with long conversation about our sisters, the campus food, and the weird things Sofia does with her camera. When we arrive outside my dorm building Noah drapes his blazer over my shoulders as the cold breeze hits me. He walks me up to my dorm and we get outside my door where I can already hear Sofia's music that's bound to get us in trouble.

"I had an amazing night Candace," Noah says leaning closer to me.

"Me too," I almost whisper. I lower my voice even more which I didn't think was possible. "I'm sorry about not telling you I run track."

Noah runs his hand through his hair. "Don't worry about it, as long as you promise me to see me as Noah and not some guy missing a leg."

I look him right in the eyes. "I promise." And with that he plants another kiss on my lips before I go into my dorm where I just want to scream about how amazing my night was.

# Chapter 8

"Where do you think you're going?" Sofia asks while sitting at our desk chair typing away on her laptop. She spins around in her chair when her eyes land on me slipping into my white converse. We've both finished our classes for today and Noah has just texted me that he got off of his shift at the crepe place. Ever since our wonderful night at the fancy crepe place, we've been spending a lot of time together; Not unlike Sofia, Brayden, and her camera.

"I'm going to meet Noah, he got off of his shift," I say while tying my shoes.

"Didn't you guys just hang out yesterday?" Sofia asks sitting crossed legged in the now wobbly chair

A devious smirk comes across my face. "Maybe," is all I respond with.

"Maybe?" Sofia repeats playing with all the different ways she can move her eyebrows.

"Ok we did, but weren't you hanging out with Brayden yesterday too," I argue.

"We weren't hanging out, we were editing," she clarifies.

"Editing? At night with your best lip gloss on?" Living with Sofia I've learned whenever she applies layers of coconut strawberry lip gloss she's planning on leaving a layer on someone else.

"I was in the mood for coconut," she shrugs. If she was in the mood for coconut she could've bought a coconut water from the 711.

"If you say so." I get up and take my hair out of my tight ponytail that was sitting on the top of my head.

"You're letting your hair down?" Sofia asks, narrowing her eyes.

"Yeah, it's something new." Seeing her eyes focused on all of my black waves I pick my brush up off of my bed and run through each strand.

Sofia nods with her eyes still on me and her hand tapping against the spinning chair. "You must really like Noah," she says. I stop running the brush through my now smooth hair and lock eyes with Sofia.

Genuinely I say, "Yeah I do." And I mean that as Noah's blue eyes flash through my head.

Sofia nods again. "That's nice," she says. She stops tapping her hand on the arm of the chair and she plays with one of the ends of her bouncy curls.

I put my brush back on my bed and cross my arms as I look at Sofia who doesn't look her same perky self as she exchanges looks from her laptop to her chartreuse toenails. She misses me? That's why she seems sad right? Or was it that prick Brayden who might have pulled something on her.

"So what's going on with you?" I ask. There's a subtle smile on my face that I hope will somehow transfer to Sofia's and erase that indifferent look she has.

She looks up from her sparkling toenails. "Going on with me? Why would something be going on with me?"

I sit back on my bed to get a closer look at Sofia's eyes that I hope will tell me everything that's going on in her chaotic brain. "I don't know Sof, you just don't seem like your cheery self." Sofia's somewhat somber glance in one second turns defensive as she shoots not so sharp daggers at me.

"Candace, you've been watching too many romantic comedies with one dimensional female characters. Just because I'm the peppy girl doesn't mean I'm going to be the peppy girl all the time,' she snaps.

I always forget Sofia is in one of those film classes where they dissect female characters and overused tropes. Of course I remember this every time we watch a movie made before 2000 or times like now when Sofia's trying to hide her real feelings.

"Ok?" she asks a bit simply.

"Ok," I repeat.

Sofia's sternness is of course fleeting and her normal smile that I've been waiting for creeps back. "It's also that time of the month." With that we laugh and I head out of the door.

Instead of our usual meeting place, being the cash register at the crepe station. Noah and I are sitting on a bench on the grass. Specifically we're on the lawn between my dorm building and the art department. It's a beautiful day with falling orange leaves and no sign of clouds in the sky, making his company even better.

We're deep in conversation getting to know each other when I ask, "So do you have a Sofia?" I can already see the confusion rising in Noah's brows at my poorly worded question.

"Not on me no," he says.

"I meant to say, do you have a best friend? Like someone who's always by your side?"

"I have friends, but not one who holds such a prestigious position I guess." Noah smirks and it's probably because I'm just staring into his eyes. I truly believe people look at him before they get contacts just to get the right shade of light blue.

"What about a roommate? Do you have one of those?" That's an easier question.

"Sadly I don't, I live off campus, but I always thought it would be nice to be in a Joey and Chandler situation."

"Having a roommate is nice. There's not that much space, but I like it."

"I'm sure you do. You and Sofia seem pretty close, like-"

Doing what I've been doing a lot now with Noah I finish his thought and say, "Rachel and Monica."

Noah shakes his head. "No I was going to say Felicity and Amy, since they were in college." He gives me that smart look and we're back in our special bubble.

"You watched Felicity?" I ask thinking of the old show.

"I told you I have older sisters." He does a little shrug. "And it wasn't a bad show."

"But it had a terrible ending," I argue. 13 year old me who was disappointed by the Felicity series finale now completely takes over my body.

"The ending wasn't that bad," Noah says with a shrug. How could he be saying this?

"What! It was terrible," I argue. I can feel we're about to have the same argument I've had several times with my mother, but stopping me from coming up with a strong claim my eyes wander over to the pathway at the edge of the sprouting grass. Walking along the pathway is a mom rolling a large stroller with a squeaky wheel. Beside her is a little girl with pigtails, just passing above the woman's ankles.

Her small voice is what catches my eye. "Mommy look at him!" she whines and points her little finger right at Noah and I. The woman who the girl is trying to summon exchanges looks from us to her daughter. She whispers something I can't make out and hurries along as her baby cries in her stroller. I don't realize how long I've been looking at the woman and daughter until Noah takes hold of my attention by lightly placing his finger under my chin making us lock eyes again.

"Don't worry about them," he whispers and presses his lips against mine. They're soft and distract me from the little girl and anyone else who might be walking along the pathway. I never thought I would be part of one of those annoying couples in the middle of the campus.

Before Noah, I used to be some version of a grandma scolding PDA like a vegan in a delicatessen, but now I'm in the delicatessen. Surprisingly, it is quite nice.

Noah and I back away from our embrace when all my nerves make me pull away. I smile with the leftover Chap Stick I have, and Noah does what he did on our date and moves some of my hair behind my ears. Knowing my waves they're just going to be blown back in front of my face, but I appreciate the gesture.

We spend some more time talking before Noah says, "Candace, I would love to talk more but I got to go to poetry class."

My face scrunches up. "Poetry class?"

"Yep. I'm studying to be some kind of Langston Hughes."

Honestly I say, "I've never seen you as a poetry guy." *Damn Candace remember you're only supposed to tell him compliments.*

Noah slowly gets up from the bench but not in the way that would make me feel the need to apologize or grab his wrist.

"I guess I never really use my best poetic words on you."

"Can you spare me one before you go?"

He lightens his tone as he looks down at me on the bench. "Obtuse. To be blunt or forthright." He gives me one last kiss before he begins walking along the green grass. When he reaches the end of the grass and steps foot on the pathway I squint my eyes to see the same woman and little girl walking along the pathway. In the same way she did last time the small girl points to Noah with her other hand in her mouth. Noah looks at the girl as he walks and his smile remains as he waves at the child and says hello. Even from my place on the bench I can see the confusion all over her face. The confusion that fades away as they keep on walking. The interaction doesn't bother Noah, as I watch him head into the English building. I wish I could be like him. I wish I could be unbothered by people's eyes on me.

After my little rendezvous with Noah, I don't go straight back to my dorm and instead hit the gym to take advantage of the only occupants being two middle aged women on the treadmills. They're doing that thing power walkers do and walking more with their arms rather than their legs. Needless to say, I don't follow their approach. Hearing Coach Pearson's booming voice in my head, I begin doing repetitions with the 10 pound dumbbells.

During my workout there's this motivation deep inside of me that doesn't let me take the slightest break, even for a second. A week ago I would say my desire comes from wanting to hold a golden trophy at the upcoming track meet, but as sweat covers my skin I realize the reason I'm pushing so hard. Because I'm realizing I have four working limbs that I'm blessed with. Spending so much time with Noah and being captivated by him every second I'm in his presence has made me stop fretting over the things that don't matter in life.

I wish the ladies speed walking on the treadmill could feel the same way. I wish everyone could.

"Uhh, when am I going to lose this belly fat," the woman who has legs as long as palm trees complains.

"Tom keeps buying all of this junk food, and it's turning me into an elephant," the other woman replies. Clearly she's never seen an elephant because they don't have a slightly curvy hourglass figure with honey brown hair to their waist. I have my earbuds in, but their complaining still drags on along with the sound of the treadmill. *Is this what I sound like when I complain about my mile time? God I hope not.*

"Have you seen Kylie Jenner's post baby body?"

At that comment, I don't mean to, but I drop the ten pound kettlebell on the smooth tiled floor. It slams against the superficial marble and both women turn their heads while keeping their power walking pace.

They go back to complaining on the treadmills and I leave the gym, heading to my dorm. When I get outside my room I look down at the floor mat to see a white sock all balled up. Not really thinking about how Sofia can be that messy, that she's sending her clothes out of the dorm. I open the door. *Big Mistake.*

I'm greeted by the sight of Sofia viscously making out with a guy who obviously is Brayden.

When her eyes leave Brayden and wander over to me she shouts, "Didn't you see the sock!?"

I look back at the sock. "It's on the floor," I argue.

"Well it's still there." Sofia moves away from Brayden and he turns to look at me hitting me with his dark gaze. As he smirks at me I realize why every time I see him I believe he's so familiar. I take a closer look into the way he's inches away from Sofia and hits me as they share a few glances. He's the guy on Sarah's Instagram kissing her. Before Sofia can say anything I close the door and after kicking the sock back in the dorm I head back to the track.

# Chapter 9

"Go!" Coach yells when everybody has run over to the right side of the turf. We all hustle to the other side and repeat this four more times.

"Warm up is over, get your water, and we'll start the workout in five minutes!" At those words we all disperse towards the corner of the field where water bottles are grouped together along with our gym bags. With my hands on my hips while I catch my breath, I walk to that corner alongside Devan who is a tall senior with a collection of colored track suits.

"You ready for this track meet?" He asks.

"I'm getting there, what about you?"

Devan lets out a long breath. "4 miles every day and 200s. I'm ready, but we've got a lot of competition."

"True," I say.

The five minutes Coach gives us to stretch and prepare for practice go by faster than any of us would like and we're back on the track lining up in the groups of our events. Being that I'm running in two events Coach has me doing two workouts this afternoon. Using my running calculator in my head this adds up to be 4 200s and my usual mile. I find it easier to do distance first leaving me standing in line with the distance girls on the turf while the boys are in their positions on the track.

Coach, who remains on the bleachers, blows the whistle and as the guys dart off us girls take place on the track. At this point I should be in my zone, but I see Sarah take her place in the lane next to me while she talks to the girl on the other side of her. Sofia kissing Brayden who apparently is Sarah's boyfriend has been on my mind since I walked in on them, but I didn't really consider Sarah in the equation or triangle until now.

"Uhh you know what I'm craving," Sarah whines.

"What girl," Vivian who is next to her asks. She's not even getting into position and instead making sure her t shirt falls right above her belly button.

"Maple syrup," Sarah responds smacking her lips. Vivian finally stops holding us up and gets down into position. "That cause your boyfriend is known for that stuff," Vivian says. The word boyfriend makes me snap my head to look at Sarah, but my glance becomes unnecessary when Coach's whistle blasts throughout the whole track. *Come on Candace you're running distance so you don't have to start sprinting. Just keep a moderate pace and you'll best your time and hopefully Sarah's.*

I focus on my running and breathing which stops me from giving into my urge to see where Sarah is. *Don't look Candace, it doesn't matter to where she is, keep your eyes forward. Come on, we're almost done with the first lap. You got this Candace, wait Sarah is in front of you and Vivian is on your tail, pick up the pace.*

As I increase my pace Vivian seems to slow down, but Sarah extends her red legs even wider. For the next two laps I contemplate running for myself or running to get ahead of Sarah. Either way the feeling of running is still so calming and freeing for me that the track seems to grow shorter as we run across it.

*Come on Candace last lap, you got this, remember what Sofia said. It doesn't matter where Sarah is. Her red skin does blend in with the track, but she doesn't matter. Try and be like Noah. Don't worry about what the people around you are doing.*

Keeping this thought stuck in my head like wet glue, I don't bother looking at any of the other girls. Although I do take a peek at Vivian when she stops to tie her shoes, which shows how committed she is. *Last 100 meters Candace, you got this! I've said it too many times now, but you still got this!*

As I reach the last meter I can't help myself. I look behind me to see Sarah jogging. Just as I'm about to cross the clean white lines my head drops, seeing Sarah glide past me again. To make it worse after Sarah runs past the finishing line Coach awards her with a high five that actually sounded like it hurt.

When I come past the line finally ending my gathering of anxious thoughts Coach exchanges looks with the screen of his stopwatch. "5:15, Candace you can do better," he says slitting his eyes.

*I know I can do better Coach, trust me I know I can do better,* I tell myself before heading to the corner of the track behind Sarah. Millions of thoughts run through my head. So I guess I haven't stopped fretting over the little things in life.

"You'll do better next time Candace," I say out loud. That was a thought. I wasn't supposed to say the words. Exhaustion does that to you.

I focus my eyes even more on the turf, but as I walk Sarah's head whips around and her eyes stab into me. The way our eyes are meeting tells me what's about to come out of her mouth won't be good.

"I know what you need to do if you want to improve," she says. She sees that she's in front of me and positions herself so that we're walking side by side.

"What's that?" I ask with a hint of defensiveness in my voice.

Sarah's smile grows and she seems to be taller now that she's right next to me. "You need to stop binging on those disgusting crepes in the cafeteria," Sarah answers with a laugh. I stop myself from responding in fear I will blurt out something stupid. I've never been the best at comebacks. If I ever thought of some they would come into my brain like 30 minutes when the confrontation was so over. Still I need to do or say something to stop myself from blurting out, "I saw your boyfriend kissing my roommate!"

My first reaction is to laugh and as I do this Sarah continues talking in her tone that has become quite condescending. "Seriously Candace if you're going to eat junk eat good junk like the taco station, that place is bomb." *Brayden is a cheater!*

I get back from practice and flop on my bed with my intentions being to text Noah, but I quickly undo the text I was writing when I realize he's still working. Working at the crepe station that according to Sarah should be closed down. *Whatever Sarah.*

The wind pounds on my window interrupting my time of breathing the strong scent of coconut that flows through the dorm room. Next to the sound of the powerful wind my phone vibrates with the sound of bells chiming signaling Noah is texting me. A few days ago I gave all of my contacts specific ring tones so I won't have to worry about being disappointed when my phone rings.

*Noah: hey just got off of work, should probably make some poems, but I wanna see you. Can I swing by?*

Me: Sure.

Noah texts me back only some seconds after my thumb leaves the screen. *Noah: Cool I'll be there in 15 minutes.*

I jump off of my bed and get ready. Like last time I let my hair fall on my shoulders and put on my best chap stick. When I'm done I go to sit on my bed, but the door swings open.

"What the hell?" Sofia shouts.

I try to read her expression as she slams the door behind her. "What's wrong?"

"Really? What's wrong? You're asking me what's wrong?" *What is she talking about?* I notice as she storms over to her bed her face is the color of Sarah's when she runs but I guess that comes from kissing the same guy.

"I thought you were over me accidentally walking in on you and Brayden?" At least that's what she told me when we briefly talked about it after Brayden left.

"I can't believe you Candace! You really don't know why I'm mad?" Sofia's hands land on her hips.

I shake my head. "No."

"Well you see this," she gestures to her face. "It's sunburn from waiting for you at track practice! Did you not get my text?"

I pick my phone up and scroll down to look at the notifications under Noah's name. Low and behold there's about 4 from Sofia asking me where I am.

Realizing I made her ringtone too low pitched to be heard. I say, "Oh my god Sof I'm so sorry."

"You should be," she snaps. She throws off her shoes and they stumble over to my side which doesn't satisfy Sofia as she kicks the shoes for a bit. "And why is your hair out again?" She says these words like I'm committing a crime. I try to form the words that Noah is going to stop by, but Sofia steals them. "You're going to see Noah aren't you?"

"Yeah he's coming by," I mumble. "Is that a problem?" I add.

Sofia shakes her head and just as she opens her mouth a knock hits our door. "That's him isn't it?"

I nod and Sofia snatched her camera off of her bed. She swings the door open and the sight of Noah's smile on the other side relaxes some of the tension that was clogging up this room.

"Hey Sofia," Noah says.

Sofia gives Noah a slight raise of her eyebrows and looks back at me before storming off into the hallway. I'm pretty sure she's already halfway down the hallway, but this doesn't stop me from getting up and yelling, "Wait I need to tell you something!"

I force a smile on my face, but I don't need to force my muscles any longer as I become once again captivated by Noah.

# Chapter 10

Noah slowly walks into the half messy dorm and I can see his eyes find mine.

"What's up with her?" He asks as Sofia's strong perfume is very much present in the room.

"I forgot she was waiting for me after track practice, hence the sunburn."

The guilt of leaving Sofia still remains inside of me, but in my defense she usually runs up to the track gate and reminds me she's there.

"Yikes." Noah moves more into the room and gestures to the space on my bed. "May I?" He asks.

I nod quickly and move to the side as Noah takes his place next to me. A part of me wants to offer him a pillow or something for his prosthetic, but it seems pretty pointless since Noah and his prosthetic appears comfortable. *I'm being over-sensitive, aren't I?*

I think of Sofia's words before she left and I grab the hair ties around my wrist collecting all of my hair into my favorite ponytail.

"Do you think my hair looks better in a ponytail or out?" I ask.

Noah shrugs. "I think whatever you like best is what I prefer," he says. His words remind me of my parents when me or one of my siblings asks who is their favorite. *So much neutrality.*

"Really do you not prefer when my hair is out and you can push strands behind my ears," Noah laughs and now would be a great time for him to get closer to me and take control of my crazy hair.

"I prefer whatever style makes you happy."

I shake my head. "How are you so Switzerland?"

"I'm not Switzerland, I just believe you look good in any hairstyle."

"Any hairstyle?" Clearly he hasn't seen my 4th grade photo when I decided to cut my bangs in the middle of the night. Let's just say kids should definitely not have access to scissors.

Noah moves his head from side to side as if contemplating some big decision. "Well maybe not a Mohawk, but any hairstyle that you rationally choose to wear I would find beautiful on you." I direct my smile towards my feet which aren't covered and displaying my lack of tolerance for pedicures. "What? Was that too cheesy?" Noah's voice brings our eye contact back and heat to my face.

"No it was... thank you."

"You're welcome, and I guess it is nice when I can push your hair behind your ears. It gives me an excuse to get close enough to kiss you." With those words he gets close enough for our lips to brush up against each other. I should break the one inch between us, but instead I begin to laugh.

Noah raises his eyebrows. "Too cheesy again?"

My words stumble out with my laughter. "No, no you're studying to be a poet. It's going to be your job to be cheesy."

"I'm not studying to actually be a poet, I'm just taking a class."

"Either way I'm fine with your cheesy lines, but when I was younger I was lactose intolerant."

"And you're not now?"

"If I was I wouldn't be spending so much time with you."

Noah nods. "Good point."

For some minutes Noah and I begin a conversation about all the foods we used to eat as a child and the different ways our parents raised us. I love that each conversation I have with him, I learn little details that I hardly know about my own family. His mom owns a diner, his dad is a carpenter, and every Sunday when they went to church his mom would fall asleep during the sermon. The way he talks about his family's quirks; I can see the love in his face giving him a nice blush. Then again it may not be his love for his family, but rather the effect of the evening sun shining through the window. I squeeze every detail of my boring family out of me until all the conversation had dried up and silence fills the room. I want to use my lack of words as a chance to get that kiss I laughed off, but instead I find something in the back of my head that I've wanted to talk to him about.

"You know I wish I was like you," I say and my head falls onto his shoulder.

"What do you mean?" he says.

I lift my head up even though I was just getting comfortable. "I mean, you just don't care what people think." For the first time as I look into his eyes his face wrinkles up and an urge comes over me to correct every one of my words.

I begin to clarify. "I mean like in a good way, you don't waste time asking stupid questions about your hair and when people stare at you it doesn't change your expression." Noah's usual calming and fun expression relaxes some of the bones in my body.

"People stare at me?" he asks.

My face goes blank for a moment until he smirks and I nudge him in the shoulder. "Look Candace it's simple. If you don't want to care about what people think of you, then don't." *Is it really that simple?*

"But it's so hard," I argue.

"Not when you compare your progress solely to your own."

"I guess that's true."

Noah cocks his head to the side. "You guess?"

"Fine, I know." Even though I say those words, the part of me that compares myself to Sarah won't die so easily.

"But don't you ever just sometimes, for one second even, catch yourself comparing yourself to other people."

Noah doesn't lose his resolute look and his straight posture makes his words have more meaning. "Candace I'm a guy with one leg. If I spent my time comparing myself to people I'd have a pretty shitty mindset." As Noah looks at me, I look at his prosthetic, which I haven't even noticed because like the rest of my dorm it's been outside the bubble Noah and I created. Even in my head when I first think of Noah, his blue eyes are the only thing I see.

"Well what about the small things? Like at the crepe place, do you taste other food and wish you could make something that good." *There's that smile again.*

"Yes I taste other food, at the cafeteria, but I never even think about the crepes I make when I'm eating Mr. Cortez's tacos."

I nod to myself and add up all of his responses. "I hope one day to be on your level, and never compare the bad food I make to Mr. Cortez's tacos."

Noah and I both share a laugh before our lips touch. After three kisses I get a knot in my stomach that can only be described as guilt. I have to go find Sofia, god knows she's probably somewhere getting more sunburnt and annoyed.

 I don't entirely want to, but I pull away from Noah lip's to look into his deep blue eyes.

"I have to go find Sofia," I whisper.

"I was wondering when you were going to ditch me," Noah says. I open my phone to text Sofia, but first I change her ringtone so that I can actually hear her response. I text to see where she is while trying to get my last minutes in with Noah. As I'm looking at the three gray dots under my blue text, finally a text pops up along with the constellation ringer I set for her.

*Sofia: I'm at the campus cafeteria.*

She could've at least given me a minute to think about where her favorite place on campus is.

"So where is she? The film room?" Noah asks.

"Campus Cafeteria," I respond.

Noah doesn't even let me reject his offer to walk with me and before I know it we're walking down campus towards the cafeteria. When we get inside I immediately see Sofia sitting at a table with a bowl of cheerios and her eyes on her camera.

Noah goes over to say hi to his coworker at the crepe place and I slowly approach Sofia's table.

"Are you done with crepe boy?" She snarls as soon as I walk up to her.

"You could come up with a better nickname, but no he's just over there."

Sofia sticks her red nose in the air towards the ceiling fan. "Well good for him."

I pull out the chair and sit down next to her. "I'm sorry Sofia," I say.

"How could you just mute me like that?" She stops looking at her camera and puts her harsh glare on me.

"I didn't mute you! I changed my ringtones, and I accidentally gave you the ocean buzzer which I can barely hear."

"And what did you give Noah?" This is why she is so hard to argue with, it's like she already knows everything.

"Bell chimes, but I can change that to your contact."

Sofia crinkles her face like she did when we first tried Noah's crepes. "I don't want your sloppy ringtone seconds, I just want you to answer when I text you."

"I will," I say eagerly.

Sofia turns back to looking at her camera and for some seconds the only voices I hear are from all the other tables. "So are you and Noah like official now?" Sofia asks with no eye contact. Hmm I've actually never thought about giving me and Noah's relationship a label.

"I don't know, I just know I really like being around him."

Sofia nods. "So you don't care about his prosthetic?"

I shake my head. "No I don't, why should the number of legs someone has determine how people see them?"

"Why should someone's running time determine how people see them?"

"That's not the same thing Sofia."

She takes a deep breath then turns to look at me with her hands still on the camera. "I accept your apology." *It sure took long enough because I almost forgot I apologized.*

She smiles and her face seems to be glowing more. I'm not sure if it's from her sunburn or the lights of the cafeteria. "And I think you and Noah are really cute."

"Thank you, now can we go back to the dorm? You need some aloe vera."

We both get up from the table and I give one quick hug to Noah before we begin walking back to our dorm. Sofia and I spent the night talking about random stuff in-between watching reruns of old TV shows. It was nice.

"Guess what?" Sofia says when a commercial break begins on her laptop.

I hate the guessing game, but I play along. "You're going to get the premium version with no commercials."

"No. Brayden and I finished our film and we're going to have a viewing party!"

I knit my eyebrows. "Where?"

"The student area duh, don't worry it will be fun, Brayden and I have it all worked out." When I hear Brayden's name the image of Sarah and Brayden kissing pops into my head.

"What's wrong?" Sofia asks.

"I have to tell you something about Brayden."

Sofia doesn't seem to register what I just said and she keeps smiling. "What is it?"

"Br-" As I'm about to ruin her relationship, my phone buzzes with Noah's name and the corresponding bell chimes.

*Noah: Gonna be working all day, just want to let you know. I hope you have a great day.*

Sofia's curls compromise my vision and she moves closer to me and looks at my screen.

"Well isn't that the cutest," she says.

"So what did you want to tell me about Brayden?"

My mind goes blank and Noah's text erases all my previous thoughts. "Nothing. I hope he's a good editor," is all I say before we go back to watching TV.

# Chapter 11

When I spend time with Noah, time goes by faster than it's ever seemed to move before. Every second, minute, and sentence counts when I'm with him; whether it's when I'm ordering a plain Jane crepe or trying to get Sofia's camera out of our faces. Time goes by so fast, that I've forgotten about what I have to tell Sofia, my need for some new running shoes, and to tell my parents about the upcoming track meet. I know I'll get to those things soon, but for now, it's nice being with Noah.

"So is Noah coming with you tonight," Sofia says. We only have some minutes before our classes start and she's just starting to get ready. Me on the other hand; I'm already dressed and holding my laptop case.

"What's tonight?" I ask.

Sofia shoots me daggers and stops putting on her ear rings. That's all she needs to do for me to remember today is her and Brayden's viewing party in the student lounge. Quickly I begin to fix the mess I made with those two words. "I'm kidding, I'm kidding. Of course he's coming."

Sofia goes back to putting on her earrings and she seems to lighten up which is hard to tell because her face is still kind of sunburned.

"Good. The more people the better."

"So I know you've been filming like every day, but exactly what will we be watching tonight?"

While Sofia is jumping into her jeans she says, "You guys will be watching my film." *Duh.*

"Yea, but what is this film about? Am I in it? Or did you edit me out?"

"It's just a film about life." *How specific.*

"Yeah but what about life?"

Sofia walks over to where I sit on my bed and puts her hand on my shoulder. "Candace don't worry about it now, just enjoy it tonight."

I should tell her filmmakers actually release trailers, but I just settle and say, "Ok, but a synopsis or at least a genre would be nice."

"A film about life. That's my synopsis."

Sofia finishes getting ready and we head to our classes which also seem to go by really fast unless one of our professors is in the mood for a double lecture. If that's the case then seconds feel like long hours of taking notes. Fortunately for me I don't have to endure any of that and after a surprise announcement about a test coming up, I head to track practice. Sofia isn't waiting in the bleachers today as she has a film study class so I don't have a hype girl to cheer me on as I run. It's kind of a bummer, but I guess I am my own hype girl with all the thoughts that flood my head when I hit the track.

Just like my time with Noah these track practices have been going by pretty fast too. Probably because the track meet isn't that far away.

I finish my sprints and eventually do my mile without looking at Sarah or Vivian. After coach has gathered us to remind us to be on our A game, I find a place on the turf and begin stretching.

"Sarah you wanna get in an extra gym session tonight?" Vivian yells as they also begin stretching. Something we only really do in detail when coach shouts at us to be on our A game.

Sarah does the flamingo stretch without bouncing. "Can't. I got to get some time in with Brayden before he has his stupid viewing party for a short film, but after would be cool so I have an excuse not to come."

My eyes widen and I jump up from doing my butterfly stretch. *Ugh I've got to tell Sofia tonight.*

After practice I get ready at my dorm, then head to the student area which is another hangout spot on campus not too far from the cafeteria. When I walk in, Sofia is the first person I see. She's side by side with Brayden hovered over a laptop that's in front of the student area's flat screen.

"Candace, yay you're here!" she squeaks when she sees me. I give a little wave to Brayden and don't speak to him much through the preparation of the viewing party. Some of Sofia's film friends show up and go on about all the movies that shouldn't have been made. I'm not even focused on Sofia's friends who are just like her, and instead my attention goes to the door when Noah walks in holding a bouquet of sunflowers. All the girls sitting with me on the student lounge couch turn their heads to look at him.

"Aww are those for me?" Sofia gushes when she looks up from her laptop.

As I approach Noah he looks from me to Sofia. "Well they're for both of you since you are roommates," he says and hands me the flowers.

"Thank you," I whisper and wrap my arms around him.

Our hands intertwine and Noah actually joins the film girl's conversation without needing to use a fake smile.

When the flat screen TV has finally turned on and our crowd are the only people in the student lounge, Brayden sits on a nearby stool and Sofia stands in front of the TV.

"Thank you everyone for coming to my viewing party, this is my short film that I've been working on called 'How Sofia Sees Life.' I hope you enjoy!" Sofia says. We all applaud and she presses a button on the remote in her hand turning the TV on. As Sofia rushes to sit next to Brayden and the lights are dimmed we all watch various scenes that were taken on campus. There's not much of a plot and it is mostly just clip after clip, but I cringe when I see myself on the screen.

"You look cute," Noah whispers, but I hardly believe him.

On screen, Sofia and I are sitting in our dorm, but the angle indicates that the camera is hidden making me shoot a glare to smiling Sofia.

"Sometimes we have to share our harsh opinions," Sofia narrates over the scene.

"So do you care about him having a prosthetic," Screen Sofia says.

All the hair on me stands up and I can feel Noah's expression change, and for the first time I wish we weren't so close.

I remember the answer I told Sofia, but my heart races while I look at myself on the screen. "Yes I do," screen me says, just as my face is obscured by subtitles.

Noah moves some inches away from me, and I just want to hide my face. "To each its own," Sofia narrates and for a second everyone in the room gives me a glance.

For the rest of the film, I can hardly watch. I just stare at Sofia, wanting an answer for what I just saw. I don't get one though and before I know it the film ends. All of Sofia's friends are hugging her before leaving.

"Noah I didn't-" I began to speak, but Noah stops me and gets up.

"Candace I have to go."

I want to grab his hand, but he's gone before I even reach. *I want to scream.*

My skin is hot. I jump off the couch to stare down Sofia who is still smiling for some reason.

"So did you like it?" She asks getting up from her seat.

"Did I like it? You've got to be kidding me, what the hell was that?"

"It was a documentary short film, duh."

I place my hands on my hips. "It was you making me look like some shallow piece of garbage in front of Noah."

Sofia acts surprised. "Oh that scene, yeah sorry about that, we needed to spice it up." *She has to be kidding!*

"So you made me look evil for spice? I can't believe you!" At this point my voice has reached its highest point and my body is having spasms like I just ran a mile.

Sofia crosses her arms. "Wait you're actually mad?"

"Yes Sofia I'm actually furious, how am I going to explain that to Noah?"

"Oh my god. All you talk about is Noah. You weren't even watching the film, you were just busy being by his side and smelling those flowers." Sofia begins pacing in the small space of the lounge. "All you care about is him. You wear your hair down for him, and you don't even thank me for being the reason you guys are together!"

Sofia's voice is now at the same level as mine. "Maybe I wanna spend time with Noah because he doesn't always film me and he certainly doesn't change my words to 'spice things up'."

Sofia stares at me with a scowl. At this moment seeing her pink skin I remember what I've been needing to tell her, and I let it spill out of me.

"Brayden is dating Sarah, so he's not just a crappy editor, but a crappy person." *I don't know if saying that was worth it.*

Sofia's face doesn't change and she barely shakes her head. "I know, and I was waiting for you to tell me. I guess I'm not the only one who screwed up."

With that Sofia storms out of the lounge leaving me standing alone wondering which one of us is a worse person. *Probably me.*

# Chapter 12

It's been some days since the viewing party and time has slowed to a crawl. The time I used to spend texting back and forth with Noah is now replaced by me staring at my phone waiting for him to answer the five apologies I've sent. The moments of Sofia and I laughing and giggling while talking or watching TV have disappeared. Now, even though we live together in a dorm the size of a walk in closet, we barely exchange a word. All of Sofia's clothes that wandered on my side, she's thrown in a messy pile on her side to make sure there is a clear line. No Noah, No Sofia, and I find myself doing nothing but looking at clocks and waiting for the day to be over.

After I change into my pajamas, I flop on my bed and open my messages. Nothing but a text from Verizon telling me I'm almost out of data, and my mom saying the same thing with questions about what I'm doing on my phone. *Everything sucks.*

It's only approaching 8pm, but I might as well take Coach's advice and get a full night's rest in preparation for the track meet. I turn the lamp off on my nightstand and stuff my face in my pillow hoping to see something exciting in my dreams.

I drift off for about 10 minutes before I hear the sound of the door crack open, and the fluorescent lights blind my eyes.

I jump up from the bundle of sheets I've wrapped myself in and look at the door where Sofia stands. She looks like she was just smiling, but when we make eye contact her green eyes are extremely harsh.

"You're going to bed this early?" She asks. Great, at least we're talking. Those are her first words to me in the past few days.

"Yes, I have to get ready for the track meet," I say.

Sofia moves over to her bed, but her eyes are still on me. "How's sleeping more than 8 hours going to help you?" she asks.

"People have more energy when they're better rested, it's a proven fact," I say as sternly as possible.

Sofia doesn't respond and kicks her shoes off along with her polka dot socks. As she squints at the nail polish on her toes it hits me that I'm probably not going to get those extra hours of rest.

"How long are you going to be up?" My words sound weird as I hold back my yawn.

Sofia does a version of a huff and a sigh. "Don't worry. I'm going to be sleeping over at one of my film friend's dorms so you can get all the grandma sleep you want." *So why did you take your shoes off?*

I flop back on my pillow and stare at the pale white ceiling. I don't know how I'm going to fall asleep now with Sofia's strong perfume lingering around my nostrils. Not too long ago the scent was comforting, but since Sofia's viewing party, the scent has landed on the list of aromas I can live without. It's right under the smells of dirty convenience stores, sour cream, and the cologne my dad used to wear to impress my mother.

Sofia still is barefoot and looking at herself in her compound mirror, poking at her eyelashes.

"So how long are you going to take?" I ask.

She does that huff and sigh combination again. "However long I need to get ready," she snaps.

Feeling her hostility I turn the lamp off and smash my head into the pillow. This bliss where the lights are off and I'm seconds away from sleeping goes away when the lights come back on.

I turn my head to Sofia and she's standing by the light switch next to the door with a smirk.

"I'm not done yet," she snaps and goes back to her bed. I want to play the game where we both keep on turning the lights on and off, but Sofia already has the upper hand since I don't feel like getting up. For the next few minutes I face the wall only listening to the loud sounds Sofia makes between searching through her dresser, doing her hair, and typing vigorously on her phone. Of course she's being passive aggressive with her ringer on. Letting me hear everyone text her back in her group chat.

After Sofia talks to her friend on an obnoxiously loud level, the door slams with the lights still on. Honestly I'm more bummed she didn't bother switching the lights off than I am about her not saying goodbye or at least giving me a wave.

The next morning I wake up before my phone alarm and thanks to the extra hours of sleep, I have quite a spring in my step. So much so that I actually put effort into doing a morning stretch session with no Sofia to distract me. I've actually come to the conclusion that without Sofia, I get things done.

Still if Sofia was here and we were in good standing, she wouldn't let me spend 15 minutes typing more apologies to Noah that he won't respond to. And why should he respond? Sure it was terrible editing at fault, but I made a promise to see him as more than a guy with a prosthetic. I broke that promise, not just because of the video, but because of all the times I've tried to stand on the side of Noah's prosthetic so people wouldn't gawk at him. These actions were usually subconscious, but if I noticed them then he likely did too.

I try my best not to think about it until I'm done running. I find myself to be the first person on the track. Coach isn't even here yet, and instead of hearing all the worries about the upcoming track meet, I hear the pleasant sound of the wind running through the palm trees. This must be the sound in that special place that therapists tell you to go to.

"Candace why are you here so early?" Coach's voice booms.

I turn from my spot in the center of the field to see Coach walking towards me carrying a water bottle in each of his hands. "I had nothing better to do, plus I wanna get ready for the track meet."

Coach opens his large bottle and takes a sip before he gets closer to me. "Really? So you're not here so your friend can film me," he says.

He probably won't have that problem anymore. "Nope, I'm here to make sure I'm my fastest at the meet."

Coach doesn't miss a beat. "You mean your best?"

My tone changes to the one I use with my mother when she corrects me. "I mean my best," I mumble. Coach continues walking, and when I hear his voice again I catch up to walk beside him.

"You want to do your best? Give me five strides across the field."

"Oooh early practice," I say excitedly,

Coach looks down at me with his resting scold. "This is not an early practice, it's an extra practice."

"But I came early," I argue.

Coach moves his head from side to side. "Aww Candace your highness, I'm sorry. You came early, so you can take it easy and just stretch." His fake light hearted tone disappears. "And give me five strides!" *Yeah I expected that.*

With coach watching from the silver bench on the side of the field, I run my strides and just like always when I run, my thoughts flow through my mind easily. *Let's go Candace, don't got Noah, don't got Sofia, but guess what you still have the track and even better you have coach, and no one to film you constantly. Now you can let out a fart without fearing it will be shown in all the AMC theaters.*

"Good, now what do you want to work on first, your mile or your sprints?"

"My mile," I say immediately.

Coach nods and instead of standing on the other side of the field while I get in my position he has me do 16 100s. The same amount of running as a mile, but because 100s are so short they seem easier.

"Come on Candace, 7 more to go," Coach yells. I take advantage of every second I get on the track to release my anger. The anger that's been building up inside my legs and palms. This is why I love running. Not because it keeps me in shape, but because there's some sense of freedom that comes over someone when they're sprinting as fast as they can, and using every muscle in their body.

After practice, I walk along the campus path alone. It only takes five minutes of walking with the rhythm of my heartbeat to pass my dorm building and head in the direction of the campus cafeteria. *You're doing this because you're hungry, but then again Noah does deserve an apology in person.*

I get to the cafeteria and push the doors open to scan the crowded space for any sign of Sofia's bouncing curls. If I'm going to apologize to Noah, it's better if Sofia doesn't witness it.

She doesn't appear to be at any one of the long wooden tables and I don't hear her squeal, so I continue maneuvering through the cafeteria. When the lights of the cafeteria grow dim, I know I've made it to the back. There's nobody sitting at the tables as usual and the only sounds that can be heard are the humming from the air vent.

Standing at the cash register is the middle aged woman I encountered last time I wanted to be daring with Noah.

"Hi, I don't know if you remember me, but I'm Candace. I'm Noah's friend," I say.

The woman looks me over with her small brown eyes that resemble buttons and crosses her broad arms.

"And," she says harshly.

I use the opposite tone of hers. "And I was kind of hoping I could talk to him about something."

The woman lets out a noise that could be mistaken for a laugh. "I don't think Noah wants to see you right now sweetie." *I guess he told her.*

She doesn't actually seem like the most open person to share your relationship problems with.

"Are you sure?" I ask, keeping my fake smile.

"Yes I'm positive, I saw his face that night after he went to your little friend's party, and I just know you messed up. I'm psychic like that." Like Sofia does, she continues to scold me until I leave.

"Thanks anyway," I mumble.

As I walk away, I take one more look at the crepe station and try to imagine Noah standing behind the cash register smiling at the small amount of people in line. Unfortunately, all that comes to mind is Noah's unhappy face at the viewing party.

# Chapter 13

"Come on I'm hungry," Devan says as we approach the doors of the cafeteria.

"Fine," I say even though I really would rather go back to my dorm. Although if I did that, I would be sitting on my bed with only furniture to keep me company.

Devan walks by my side greeting the people we pass, while I scan the area in hopes of seeing a familiar face that doesn't hate me. I don't stop looking around until my eyes fall on Sofia who is sitting with the student council, amongst a bunch of laptops and coffee cups.

Devan, oblivious to the tension between Sofia and I, exchanges looks between us and says, "You wanna sit with Sof, or are you tired of seeing your roommate all the time?"

Sofia has been sleeping in her friend's dorm for the past few days and I've sort of enjoyed having a single room despite the lack of her company.

As the days go by, my anticipation for the track meet keeps me going, and it's what has stopped me from trying to contact Noah a thousand times a day. I didn't see him a lot around campus before, but now he's fallen off the face of the earth. He has somehow found a way to work at the crepe station, but not be there the second I step into the cafeteria.

I look at Sofia as she takes a sip of her green juice. "You go. I'm going to find something to eat."

Devan goes over to Sofia's table and I make my way in between all of the tables and stations. As I'm about to make my way over to Mr. Cortez's taco station, a girl from track pops up. I recognize her as Hannah who is running the 800. Saving me she says, "Candace you wanna sit with us?"

I scan the table of people I've never seen before typing on their laptops and occasionally exchanging looks between each other. I nod and sort of wish I brought my laptop instead of having my gym bag slung over my shoulder. Hannah lets me share a paper bowl of chips and we talk about track while she ignores the writing she was doing in her notebook. We mostly talked about track, and when there was nothing else to mention about the hurdle crisis of 2016, she went back to writing. As the conversations everyone is having circle around me, my eyes land on the cafeteria doors.

I contemplate going through those doors, but I stop myself when I catch an interesting conversation going on at the end of the table.

"That crepe station over there is so depressing," a girl with red bangs comments.

"Yeah they should just get rid of it, and I don't know replace it with another sushi spot," a guy responds while still typing on his laptop.

I want to say something in defense, but nothing they are saying isn't true.

"Another sushi spot would be amazing," Hannah agrees and takes the last chip from the bowl we were sharing. *We weren't really sharing to be honest, I ate like five chips.*

"That guy who runs the place is kind of cute," Another girls says. And now she and the table have all of my attention.

Another girls speaks up. "Yea but he has a prosthetic, and every time I see him I think of the joke; what's an amputee's favorite breakfast spot?"

Everyone at the table says, "IHOP," in unison and I get angrier than I probably should over such an old dumb joke.

Their laughter continues and I can't control my body as I jump out of my seat. "You guys are assholes," I shout. Surprisingly, only a few tables have turned their attention towards me.

"What it's just a joke," the girl with the red bangs says still laughing.

"Well it's a stupid joke," I say.

"Someone's uptight," the girl at the other end of the table whispers.

"And someone's bad at whispering," I snap back. The only sounds at the table are from the guy trying to type and hide his face in his laptop. He's not the only one who doesn't want to look at me, everyone else turned silent and stared at their sushi. Seeing their embarrassed faces, I make my way over to the door, but stop when I see Sofia's green eyes glued to me.

I quickly look away from her and head to Mr. Cortez's taco station, which happens to have no line. Mr. Cortez, a small elderly man, stands behind the cash register with a warm smile.

"Whoever you just stood up for is lucky to have you, now what would you like?"

*I can't imagine lucky is how Noah feels.*

# Chapter 14

"I'm spending the night here. I'd ask if that's ok with you, but then again this is still my dorm," Sofia announces when she walks into the room. She has her duffel bag slung over her shoulder and she doesn't look at me as she goes straight to her dresser. I was wondering when she was going to run out of clean clothes and find her shirts spread out across her side of the room.

"Glad to have you back," I say.

My voice is laced with sarcasm, but I try to hold it back. It is kind of nice to have her back, but I wish she would leave her attitude at the door.

Sofia bursting into our dorm in the middle of the day when I'm trying to study for chemistry isn't ideal, but I go back to burying my nose in my textbook hoping that will drown out the awkwardness. I continue going over my notes and rereading several paragraphs on covalent energy almost putting myself to sleep. I'm so tired of looking at the small handwriting in the textbook that my face literally hits the pages of the book. The smell of the glue binding the new textbook attacks my nostrils and snaps me out of my daze only to bring me right back to reading the same paragraphs.

"Chemistry hmm," Sofia mumbles. I turn to look at her and she's laying on her bed with her phone sitting right on her stomach.

"Yup very interesting material," I say.

I probably should've said something else because Sofia's face is still sternly glaring, but maybe that's because her face has just gotten accustomed to being that way. I think she's going to say something else, but she doesn't, so I go back to doing my version of studying. When I've read a whole page about Lewis Dot Structures and bonds there's a knock on our door. I almost forget Sofia is in the room and for a moment I think it's her. She's not the type of person to knock, especially when it comes to our dorm door.

"I got it," Sofia says.

With my eyes only slightly on my textbook I watch Sofia walk over to the door and swing it open.

Brayden stands on the outside leaning on the doorway with his left arm. "Why aren't you dressed? I texted you 5 minutes ago," he snaps.

"Well I'm sorry I don't check my phone every 5 seconds." *Hmm it seems like someone should owe me an apology about me not seeing her messages.*

"So are we still going?" Brayden asks and heads into the room. His strong cologne follows him.

"I mean… what time does the exhibit start? I have some studying to do," Sofia argues.

Brayden moves his hand off of the doorway and crosses his arms.

"So I'll take that as yes, be out front in 5," he says.

Brayden saunters down the hall, and Sofia just slams the door making some of her posters vibrate. I've lived with Sofia for a long time, and even though we're in a bad place I'm still surprised she puts up with Brayden.

I let this thought leave me while Sofia quickly gets ready before heading out the door. I use this time after the door slams to check my text messages from Noah and I compose another one thinking he can't ignore them forever.

*Noah I'm really sorry, I just want you to know I don't care about you having a prosthetic, I'm sorry I broke your promise. I really wanna see you again.*

When I'm done typing the words I quickly delete them and go to the window of my dorm. I stare at the fall leaves crumbling on the ground and in the trees, and as my eyes are glued to the outside I see a buggy breeze by in the parking lot. It's not light blue like Noah's, but it sure reminds me of him.

................

"Do you think this is all worth it?" Devan asks. We're both done with our track workouts and sitting on the bleachers looking at the empty field. Something that is really nice to do when it's not too hot and there is no trash or anyone in the stands.

I turn to him after drinking a sip of my water. "Do I think what is all worth it?" I ask.

Devan does a combination of a shrug and headshake. "You know just working so hard for track and trying to get straight A's."

*Hmm, that's a pretty deep question. Exhaustion does that to you.*

I don't think about the question all that much. "Yeah I guess it's all worth it, you know, getting that feeling of relief when you cross the finish line."

"But shouldn't we be enjoying the whole experience and not just waiting for the end."

I shrug. "I enjoy the whole experience, the running, the working out, it all makes track what it is," I exclaim.

Devan sighs. "This is a dumb conversation to have when we've just finished running."

"True," I say and we sit in silence for a bit.

"So have you talked to Noah since the whole thing," Devan asks, drastically changing the subject. His comment makes me that I regret telling him everything that happened with me and Noah.

I shake my head. "No, I miss him though," I say honestly.

"Then you should talk to him, It's not like you did anything wrong. Brayden was the one who edited the dumb film."

"Yeah, but I don't know. I just don't feel right about it. I believe I would make him uncomfortable." I shrug.

Devan releases another sigh. "I feel bad for him, you know the way people give him all of those pity looks."

I almost choke on the water I was attempting to drink. "Are you talking about Noah? He does not want anyone to feel bad for him, and that's what I love about him. He lives his life apart from other people's perceptions, and that's refreshing when most people live only thinking about how they're seen rather than who they actually are."

"He sounds like a great guy." Devan turns from looking at the track to looking right at me. "And you're glowing girl, that's a sign saying you should stop hanging with me and go talk to him. "

I try to hold back the heat rising in my complexion. "You think so?" I ask.

Devan nods and we exchange goodbyes before I head in the direction of the cafeteria. It takes me a few minutes, but eventually I make my way inside and maneuver over to the crepe station. It's still pretty abandoned, but bringing light to the area is Noah standing behind the counter, looking as cheery as always.

I walk slowly, but I get to the counter where Noah and I are face to face. Some sort of uneasiness comes over him, but he stays in the same spot looking at me.

He seems to be about to say something, but my words come first. "Noah I'm so sorry, I just want you to know Brayden edited that thing in the film and I don't feel that way at all. I miss you, I really miss you."

Noah again looks like he's about to say something, but a woman's voice booms from the back of the station. "Noah come help me lift this bucket of fake chocolate!"

She makes me think about the taste of the crepes, but at this point I actually miss their rubbery charm.

Noah finally speaks. "I'm sorry Candace I've got to go."

His voice is still nice and smooth and he goes to the back of the station leaving me by the counter. It was worth a shot.

I walk out of the campus cafeteria to see Sofia walking out of the cafe with her arms crossed. She seems sad, and she's not scolding me at all.

"He's still not talking to you?" she asks.

I don't know how she knows what happened, but I say, "Nope."

"I'm sorry about everything," she whispers and gets closer to me. "I was being so stupid."

She comes beside me and we subconsciously begin walking. "You were? I hadn't noticed."

Sofia shoots me a glare. "You wanna know why I told Brayden to do it?'"

*I've been waiting.* "Umm yeah."

"Because I was kind of jealous of you spending so much time with Noah and him having so much of an influence on you."

I hold back some laughter, "Really?" *I can't imagine Sofia being jealous of anyone. Then again, I can totally see it.*

"Yeah, but I screwed up. You guys *were* really cute together, but I should be saying you guys *are* cute together."

The pep that I missed from Sofia is back in her voice bringing a smile to my face.

We walk some more before I say, "I'm sorry for not telling you about Brayden and Sarah."

Sofia nods. "It's cool, and I dumped Brayden at the exhibit."

The words fly out of my mouth. "Thank God!"

Sofia smiles at me. "So are you going to try to get back with him?"

"I don't think he wants that," I admit.

"Well I'm glad to help you," Sofia says.

With that Sofia wraps her arm around me, and we head towards our dorm.

# Chapter 15

Sofia has unpacked her duffel bag and she no longer scolds me with vengeance. We're back to talking excessively, saying goodbye to each other, and most importantly eating lunch in the cafeteria together. It kind of sounds like we're in high school and with the drama that occurred over the past weeks, one wouldn't be too far off in assuming that we were. Our relationship has also improved from a lack of recording devices. Now Sofia is actually spending less time looking at the camera and more time helping me come up with some way to win Noah back. We've watched several romantic comedies, studied the resolutions, and went over every text I sent Noah. We spent most of our time dissecting the messages I probably shouldn't have sent.

"I think Noah is making too big of a deal about this," Sofia says opening up our picnic basket on the green grass.

"That's easy for you to say. You're kind of the reason he's not talking to me," I snap back.

Sofia responds by nudging me on the shoulder. "Hey, you said we were over that."

I put my hands up. "You're right, you're right, I'm over it, but I don't think he's making a big deal about it. I think he is making an appropriately sized deal about things."

Sofia shoots me that infamous glare of hers. "Really? Come on Candace, you didn't do anything if you think about it. I watched the short film over and over again, and honestly Brayden is as shitty an editor as he is a guy." Well I already learned that information at the film party.

I shrug just a little and hide my answer by taking a bite of my sandwich. "Ok maybe he's taking this a little harder than the average person, or maybe he's over it and he just lost interest in me."

Sofia growls, "Don't do that!" she snaps.

"Do what?" I ask.

"Excuse his actions by making it sound like what happened was your fault."

"Well, I'm sorry it's just a possibility," I argue.

Sofia's voice gets harsher. "No it's not Candace! You're amazing, beautiful, and hardworking any guy especially Noah would be happy to have you."

We both lock eyes. "Thank you Sof, you know you're one of the best people I know. Even when we were slamming doors on each other I missed you."

For a moment we both laugh and hug before going back to thinking about Noah and any words I can somehow say to help the situation. When we're done I head back to my dorm and take a long nap. When I wake up, I suddenly have the energy to talk to Noah. I don't know exactly what I'm going to say, but I'm sure the first sentence that comes out of my mouth will be: Noah please talk to me. *Hopeless begging, that will get him for sure.*

I walk into the cafeteria slowly, but not slowly enough because I quickly end up at the cash register looking at the empty crepe station. This time, there is no Noah to brighten the dusty counter and crepe ingredients that are under the usual lights. I don't move or yell out Noah's name, instead I keep looking around the station and eventually I begin counting all the blueberries there are in a small container. I don't stop counting the almost molding blueberries until Noah's eyes come into my view.

"Hey," he says looking from me to the cash register.

I'm suddenly reminded of the first time I met Noah standing in front of the station.

"Hey," I repeat not wanting to scare him off. I look down at the counter before our eyes meet. Instead of asking if we can talk, an idea comes to my mind as I scan the crepe menu. "I wanted to say how sorry I am, by ordering the chocolate deluxe crepe," I say, already feeling the pain in my stomach. The chocolate crepe is the worst on the menu with the most industrial, artificial ingredients. When we were spending time together Noah told me he had only made one once, when Sofia and I ordered it, and it almost made him throw up.

Noah smiles, but only to himself. "I can't let you do that Candace," he practically mumbles.

For a moment I consider his words, "The customer is always right," I say smoothly.

Noah nods, and I'm honestly hoping he'll back down, "One chocolate deluxe crepe coming up," he says. *Is he even worth it?*

Noah gets straight to it and before long there is an interminable pile of brown on the plate in front of me. I don't take it back to one of the tables and instead pick up a fork from the counter. I move with the fork in my hand like I'm in a stop motion picture, and just as it stabs the middle gushy part Noah laughs.

"Candace I can't let you do this," he says. He comes over to where I stand with the fork and he takes the tray and crepe before throwing it in the trash. Surprising me, he opens the door that separates the station and the outside and gestures for me to follow him to a table. *Finally.*

We sit across from each other and I can't stop myself from spilling my guts, "I'm sorry about the movie Noah I mean it, I said no, but Brayden edited it, but that's not the point, I'm sorry for making you think I broke your promise." My last words create tears that sting my eyes and I can't stop them from falling down my face. *Candace you weren't supposed to cry.*

"Hey it's ok," he says soothingly.

I continue crying but the tears become lighter and lighter. "No it's not, you hate me and won't talk to me," I cry. My tears compromise my vision, but I see Noah helping me up and escorting us both to the outside patio where there is more space and less people. My tears quickly go away under the sunlight, and the next thing I know, Noah and I are facing each other while leaning against the walls of the cafeteria.

"I'm really sorry Noah," I say this time without whining.

Noah makes sure he looks me right in my eyes. "Look Candace, I know it was edited, but if I'm being honest I just don't like being reminded every second of the day that I'm different." He sighs a little and continues talking. "I just want people to see me as more than my physical limitations Candace, and I think you do, but sometimes it seems like you're trying too hard."

"I see you for who you are," I confirm.

"Are you sure?" he asks.

"I'm positive Noah. This might sound cheesy, but you make me not care about what people think and I like that a lot."

"So if I told you to wear your hair in a ponytail right now because it looks better, would you take that rubber band off of your wrist?"

I play with the blue rubber band he's talking about. "No, I wouldn't. I like the way my hair blows in the wind."

"Me too," Noah says quietly. "You want to know how it all started, don't you?"

"If you're willing to tell me," I say.

Noah takes a long breath and begins talking. "I'll give you the short version. When I was young I got really sick and my parents didn't really know what was going on. It just got worse every day until I could barely stand and the next thing I knew the doctor was telling me they needed to amputate," Noah stops and rubs the bridge between his eyes.

"I'm sorry," I say.

"You don't need to be," His eyes seem to become somber and I wrap my arms around him. Surprisingly he doesn't back away, and embraces my touch, which I've missed.

'So are we talking again?"

Noah smiles which is a good sign. "Yes, Candace, I'll see you around."

He turns to go back to work, and when his back is about to be facing me, I yell, "Come to my track meet this weekend?"

He turns around and hits me with that winning smile. "Ok," he says.

# Chapter 16

The bleachers are filled with people. On the field, teams are stretching a little more than usual. Not because it will actually help them all the much, but mostly just to put on a show for their competitors. Coach calls us all in to give his usual version of a pep talk before things get started.

"Listen up guys, we've been preparing for this a good amount of time, and I just want to say I'm proud of you guys even if you don't win any medals. Although if you want new gear I suggest you win all the medals, because I don't see any other way we'll get the funding." Some of us laugh and coach continues. "Anyway this is supposed to be motivating so go out there and do your best, and stay in your lane." Coach gives the side eye to Frank who tends to let his big feet wander into other lanes. After Coach's words, we all do our warm ups on the field with the other teams and as we're running my eyes drift over to the bleachers where Sofia is in the front row, packed in with the wall of people. She doesn't seem bothered by the tight seating, and she's instead smiling at everyone who walks by. There is no sign of Noah yet.

Warm ups go by quickly and when all the teams are somewhat gathered, the meet begins. "Oh my god look," Sofia says pointing towards the track. I follow her finger to the runners jumping over hurdles. It's something I've seen plenty of times, but Sofia thinks it's some kind of act at the circus. We continue watching each race, but my attention leaves the other runners when I hear the announcer's voice.

"Will the runners for the 1600 please start warming up, I repeat will the runners for the 1600 please start warming up," he says in the dullest, monotone voice.

Sofia and I exchange looks before she hugs me and says, "You're going to do great."

I get off the bleachers and as I head to the track Sarah walks beside me. I don't know what it is, but I haven't thought about Sarah in a while. I haven't thought about beating her, running ahead of her, or trying to look better in my uniform even though they're meant to be pretty unflattering.

"Hey," I say.

"Hey," she repeats.

We don't say another word as we keep walking until I turn to look at her.

"Are you nervous?" I blurt out.

Sarah smiles. "A little." She raises one eyebrow. "Are you?"

"Just a bit," I admit.

Sarah looks at the ground and then back at me. "Well, good luck."

She actually seems genuine, catching me off guard. "Good luck to you too."

After another round of warm ups and registering for a number that's now plastered on my body, all the girls running the mile are on the track and I take my position in lane 8. Before I get into my zone I look over at the silver bleachers. Sofia is alone with the crowd and a smile travels across her face. *No Noah.* I can't think about the lack of his presence now.

*Noah isn't here, but your parents aren't here either, so what's the big deal? You have Sofia. She loves you and she says you're going to do great so you have no choice but to be great. But don't do great for her or anyone else, do great for you. Look at all those people cheering, they're cheering for you! Well not really you, but it doesn't matter. First lap done. Candace doesn't this feel amazing, doesn't this feel like you're leaving all of your problems behind you. Second lap done, third lap done. Last lap Candace, come on you can do this.*

As the crowds of bleachers get louder and our pace grows quicker, sweat covers my forehead and I can feel my ponytail slinging side to side behind me. I'm running down the last 200 with no knowledge of where the other girls are. My body is moving all on its own and I only get out of my zone for one second to look at the bleachers. Something I can already hear coach yelling at me for. I don't care though, and I take a glimpse over at the bleachers. *He's there.* It only takes me a second to notice his glimmering blue eyes. Noah's sitting right next to Sofia smiling, and the next thing I know, I've cross the finish line. I hear the crowd cheer and step off the track, only to see that all the other girls are just now crossing.

*You did it Candace.*

I don't let my win sink in long, but rather I head right to the bleachers.

"You came in first place," Sofia coos and gives me a small hug. She would've really wrapped her arms around me, but I'm drenched in sweat. This doesn't stop me from approaching Noah though.

"You're here," I say catching my breath.

"Yes I am," Noah responds and gets closer to me. "And you won," he adds.

I shake my head before getting closer to him and wrapping my arms around his neck. "Not important. What's important is that I did better than my last mile."

Noah plants a kiss on my lips before replying, "You're right."

Thank you for reading my story!

There are more available on amazon.

Also, go ahead and follow me on social media to tell me how much you liked this book! Unless you didn't like it, in which case you should follow my social media so you can tell me how much you didn't like it!

https://linktr.ee/loganeffling